Convince My Heart

MADDIE JAMES

SAND DUNE BOOKS

Convince My Heart

Maddie James

About Falls Mountain

Welcome to Falls Mountain, and the quaint town of Harbor Falls.

Tucked deep into the Blue Ridge Mountains, bricked streets, lakeside views, and charming local shops set the scene for small town romance.

In this standalone-but-interconnected series, you'll meet bakers, bookstore owners, chocolatiers, teachers, and more—all trying to run their businesses, chase their dreams, and keep their hearts in check. But in Harbor Falls, love has a habit of showing up unannounced...

From second chances to secret babies to grumpy-sunshine pairings, each book brings a satisfying happily-ever-after and a cast of characters you'll want to visit again and again.

Falls Mountain Romance is a companion series to the Sweet Hart Inn Romance books by Maddie James.

Convince My Heart

***She rescued a stray cat... but it might be her own heart
that needs saving.***

Dr. Caleb Wyatt thought opening a veterinary clinic in the
quiet town of Falls Mountain would be a dream come true.
Instead, he's drowning in chaos—Mrs. Pierson's poodle has a
dating problem, a colicky calf keeps him up at night, and his
office looks like a zoo gone rogue.

Enter Samantha "Sammi" Jamieson, an administrative
assistant with a soft spot for rescue animals—and one particularly mischievous cat. She's only at the clinic for a checkup,
but when she sees how much help the new vet needs, she steps
in to lend a hand.

What starts as a temporary job soon turns into something
more. Between the purrs, paw prints, and unexpected sparks,
Sammi wonders if she's rescued more than just a cat. But
falling for the charming, disorganized vet wasn't part of her
plan—and she's sworn off love for good reason.

Caleb's not giving up without a fight. Convincing her to

stay was easy. Convincing her to open her heart again? That's the real challenge.

Especially after she uncovers something about his past that has her keeping her distance.

Convince My Heart is a sweet, small-town romance filled with furry friends, heartfelt moments, and a slow-burn love that feels like coming home. Perfect for readers who love:

- A compassionate, slightly chaotic hero,
- A guarded heroine with a soft heart,
- Found family and small-town charm,
- Animal antics and happily-ever-afters.

Chapter One

A woman knows when a man is staring at her. It's a sixth-sense sort of thing. And Samantha Jamieson knew that the man behind her in the grocery checkout line at the Ralph's Grocery Store was staring a hole through her back.

Gulp.

Stifling a sideways glance, she carefully placed her selected items on the counter: a half gallon of milk, a soft drink, a square pack of American cheese slices, three cans of cat food, a box of tampons. A disconnected collection, to be sure, and she still had no clue what was for dinner. She nudged the tampons behind the milk, semi-hiding the box. Only then did her gaze drift to the left, toward *his* groceries.

Interesting.

A large hand placed a divider in front of his order—whipping cream, butter, linguini, Parmesan cheese, fresh mushrooms, a small chicken, and a few items more her brain didn't register—placed one after another onto the moving counter. Much more exciting than her choices. His hands worked back and forth. Large hands, callused hands, with long fingers. The items piled up. Her gaze traveled to his arms, to his chest, throat, face....

Eye contact!

She jerked back to stare at her own purchases. Sadly, they nicely summed up her life. Common. Plain. Boring.

"That will be sixteen-ninety-seven, Sammi," Carly Hartman, the checkout girl, announced. Sammi snapped back to look at the bubble-gum smacking teenager and fumbled in her purse for the money. Handing over a twenty-dollar bill, she kept her eyes riveted straight ahead. Her thoughts, though, were definitely still stuck on the man creating a considerable amount of heated energy beside her.

Stop it, Sammi. You don't ogle men.

Carly thrust her change and receipt forward, popped her gum, and then bagged Sammi's purchases. Risking one more peek to her left, Sammi watched the man take a step toward her. She observed him full-on as he concentrated on his items. His dark brown hair was shaggy, but not quite long enough to reach his collar. His blue jeans were dusty on his tall, lean body. His laced work boots needed a good swipe with a damp rag. She inspected him closer—he was tan, must work outdoors. Dirt showed under his fingernails—farmer? And perspiration stains on his shirt—hmm, maybe construction. He didn't seem the kind of man to buy the ingredients for Chicken Alfredo.

And what kind of man would that be, Sammi? Given your oh-so-limited experience with men? Hmmmm?

But he was handsome. Dirty and sweaty, yes—and likely tired, if the bags under his eyes were any sign—but he was about the best-looking specimen she'd seen around Harbor Falls in quite some time. Must be new in town.

List! Does he have a list?

If so, then there was possible proof of a wife. One who had

sent him to the grocery store for dinner ingredients on his way home from work.

Drat.

Sammi sneaked a closer look and noticed his hands were bare. No list, no ring, not even a thin circle of white where one would have been on that dark, tanned finger. And then she sensed more than knew that he was alone.

Just like her.

Quickly, and a bit startled where her thoughts were taking her, she took the bag of groceries from Carly and left the checkout area. If she ambled along, the man would likely follow her out of the store in a few minutes, and perhaps she could sneak another peek....

No, Sammi.

Only after depositing her bag in the back seat of her Chevrolet sedan did she glance toward the store entrance. On cue, he stepped out. Their gazes clashed again. Sammi's skittered off. Within seconds, she slipped into the driver's seat.

Fumbling in her purse, she groped for her keys and then adjusted her rearview mirror as he stepped in front of her car. Again, their gazes collided, and his skipped off this time. She slipped her key into the ignition of the Chevy.

He kept walking—past the Dodge minivan, an old Jeep Wrangler, the extended-cab pickup truck. He walked until he stopped almost two-thirds of the way down the row at an old flatbed truck.

Sammi twisted the key in her ignition.

Her brain spun. *Farmer, landscaper, construction worker.* One of those.

He put his bag of groceries inside the cab and, in almost the same motion, entered the truck and gunned the engine. The old vehicle rumbled to life—rusty red and peeling, dented fenders, a few old feed sacks tossed on the bed anchored down with a stack of two-by-fours. He pulled out and drove toward her.

Sammi fiddled with her purse again as he passed, then pulled her car out of gear and into drive. Turning the steering wheel and tramping on the accelerator, she fell into place behind him as they both headed out of Ralph's parking lot.

What am I doing? Following a perfect stranger? Why?

"Because I want to know more about a man who looks like that, drives a flatbed pickup, and cooks Chicken Alfredo for Friday night dinner," she mumbled. "Besides, what else do I have to do tonight?"

They approached the intersection, and both turned left. At the next light, Sammi's mystery man sped up and entered the right-hand turn lane. The left lane was the one Sammi needed to go home. A part of her wanted to follow. A part of her wanted to pull up beside him and say something cute like, "Need help with dinner?"

But she settled for the part that made her slow her car, flip on her left blinker, and veer toward the lane that would take her home—home to her quiet little cottage on the edge of town that was perfect for a single, thirty-something spinster. It was the part that went right along with her mousy dishwater-brown hair, her plain but comfortable sneakers, her baggy sweatpants and T-shirt, and her fingernails chewed to the quick.

He hit the accelerator again. Her mystery man turned right on red and headed toward the country.

Sammi followed the line of traffic left and headed for home, thankful for the one bit of excitement at the end of her mundane day. Fully realizing that nothing exciting was ever going to happen to her here in small town of Harbor Falls, unless she took a risk.

Not tonight, Sammi.

THE DAMNED PHONE WOULDN'T STOP RINGING.

Caleb Wyatt grimaced and rolled face-first into his pillow. Couldn't a guy get at least one uninterrupted night's sleep around here? Something had disturbed his sleep every night for the past week.

The call couldn't be about Chuck Marshall's mare. He'd delivered that foal this afternoon. He'd taken care of the Henrys' colicky calf the night before that. Tuesday was the night Mrs. Pierson's poodle got intimate with the husky next door. He'd had to calm Mrs. Pierson more than the poodle. And he believed it was Monday when Ryan Campbell's iguana turned yellow, and the child went into hysterics. Seemed his older brother told him he had yellow fever and was going to die.

Of course, the older brother had spray-painted the iguana. And the damn thing might have died if Caleb hadn't gotten the paint off in time.

Was there no peace?

What emergency awaited him tonight?

All this and he hadn't even hung out his veterinarian shingle yet—of course, word traveled fast in small towns. He'd put the ad in the paper only yesterday.

"Hullo?" The receiver barely reached his ear. Caleb glanced at his clock radio. Was it only eleven-fifteen? What early nights he was keeping lately....

"Dr. Wyatt?"

"Mmhmmmm."

"Sorry to bother you, but I saw your advertisement in the Harbor Falls Sun."

"Mmmmm."

"It's an emergency."

He arched a brow. "Oh, umhmmmm?"

"It's my cat."

Caleb opened an eye. The woman sounded anxious. "What, uh..." He cleared his throat, then propped himself up on an elbow. "What seems to be the problem, ma'am?"

"She's... I don't know. She seems to be choking."

"Did she eat something unusual?"

"I don't know!"

"Swallow a coin, a bead, a paper clip?"

"I don't think so."

"Can she breathe?"

"Yes."

"Describe what she's doing."

"Well, actually, she's sort of...gagging, and heaving. Her entire body is trembling. A raspy sound is coming from her throat. And uh, she's spitting up a bit, and making this horrible sound, and...ooh yuck! *There's this slimy gray thing coming out of her throat!*"

"Mrs...." Caleb groaned and burrowed deeper into his pillow.

"Jamieson. Miss."

"Miss Jamieson. Your cat has a hairball."

"A what?"

"A hairball."

"What's that?"

"It's perfectly normal. How long have you had the cat, Miss Jamieson?"

"About a month. She was a stray."

"Have you had her checked out?"

"Uh, no."

Caleb pinched the bridge of his nose. "Bring her by tomorrow. She's in no danger. We'll run the gamut. Shots and so on, and I'll give her something to prevent hairballs. Now if you don't mind, it's late...."

"Of course. Sorry to disturb—"

Caleb barely heard the click of the phone on the other end. His receiver never made it back to the bedside table. He didn't care. There sure were some silly people in the world. This was the first time a damn hairball had interrupted a night's sleep!

SAMMI ASSUMED SHE DIDN'T NEED AN APPOINTMENT. She hoped she'd be able to drop Dicey off at the vet early in the morning, leave so she could run some errands, then pick her up again later in the day. She called the cat Dicey because she was snow white all over, except for two large, perfectly round spots on her back. And the cat had grown so fat over the month she'd had her, that she rolled like dice when she tried to lick her belly.

Sammi hated to admit it, but the cat was growing on her. She was smitten.

She'd kept the cat on a whim, and from the urging of her friend, Emma Jo, to give the big girl a *furever* home, as she'd called it. It was a startling thought at first, being responsible for another living thing, but the idea grew on Sammi.

She had hoped the vet would finish with Dicey by the time she'd finished her errands, so she could go home and relax the rest of the afternoon. After the laundry, of course.

She'd figured wrong.

First, she had a hard time finding the clinic. There was only a small, nondescript ad in the *Harbor Falls Sun* that had given an address. That's where she'd originally found his number. *Dr. Caleb Wyatt*, it read. *Small and Large Animal Practice. 2874 Grimes Mill Road.* Then, the phone number.

There was just one problem.

She was staring at a mailbox that bore the numbers 2874. The mailbox was rusty and in need of a coat of paint, and it looked as if someone had written the numbers there with a black permanent marker. She knew she was on Grimes Mill Road, about a mile out of town and into the foothills. This had to be it, but where was the clinic? No sign, just a small frame farmhouse and a red barn against the hilly background of trees and mountains. Nothing fancy, and not at all what she'd expected.

The cat mewed in the seat next to her.

"Oh, all right, Dicey. We're here, so let's see what we can find." Sammi pulled off the main road onto the narrow gravel driveway that led to the area between the barn and the house and parked her car.

She tried the house first, knocking on the front door. No answer.

She debated whether to check the barn to find Dr. Caleb Wyatt or just run back into town where she could call a vet who actually had an office.

And she probably would have done that, too, if it hadn't been for the promise she'd made to herself the other day. The day after she'd chickened out, following her dream man out of the grocery store.

Some women wouldn't consider him a dream man, but she couldn't help herself. She'd thought of him often the past two nights. She liked his lanky look and his tanned, weathered appearance. And that he worked outdoors.

He was the total opposite of her. She was short, pale, and worked inside.

That's what made him so interesting.

And well, sexually appealing.

She'd vowed that she was going to spice up her uninteresting life, take some chances and do things a little differently. Take a risk now and then—assert herself.

She would start taking chances.

So, Sammi. Assert yourself.

She looked at the old red barn, swallowed hard, and before she realized it, walked determinedly toward it. She clutched Dicey a little firmer in her arms—she needed to get a carrier—and the plump cat squirmed.

The large wooden door stood ajar. She pushed it fully open, and its hinges squeaked. She poked her head inside.

A large red-coated animal leaped across her line of vision. Sammi bumped into the door, which forced it to open wider. A small squeal ripped from her throat. A dog barked in the corner, then lunged. Something flapped overhead. Feathers and straw swirled in the dusty air. Dicey scratched and clawed, and it was all Sammi could do to hold on to her, those back claws ripping into her shirt sleeves, until the cat wrenched herself from Sammi's arms and went sailing into oblivion.

A chicken squawked.

The cat screeched from somewhere.

The red beast howled in the corner.

Country music blared from... Somewhere.

Sammi breathed in air that smelled like manure.

Standing across the room from her, a man with a dumbfounded expression raised his voice over the cacophony. "Ah, hell. What did you have to go and do that for?"

Balking at his question, Sammi took a deep breath and glanced about. She'd entered a small room at the side of the barn. Bales of straw sat in one corner next to an open stall. She noticed that the red animal bawling was a young calf. The chicken, now quiet, looked down from a rafter. And the dog, a large black Labrador, was panting happily next to its owner.

Where is Dicey?

"I'm... I'm so sorry. I was looking for Dr. Wyatt. Do you know where he is?"

She got a good look at the man then. Shaggy hair, dusty jeans, muscular hands. Mr. Chicken Alfredo himself? Sammi's heart slammed against her chest, and she gulped.

"I'm Caleb Wyatt."

Suddenly, her mouth was drier than an apple fritter-on-a-stick at the state fair. She stammered. "I... I have this cat. I called, and now, well, she's... She jumped out of my arms and she's around here somewhere."

"I don't recall any appointments this morning."

Drat. She knew she should have called. "You said last night. We spoke on the phone—"

Recognition settled in his eyes. "Ah yes. You are the hairball."

Sammi nodded.

"I mean, your cat had a hairball," he corrected. "Somehow I forgot all about it."

"It's okay. I'll just find my cat and come back another time... Make an appointment."

Dr. Wyatt shook his head and glanced off behind the bales of straw. After a moment, he stalked across the room. Sammi watched those long, lean legs as he bent over and snatched Dicey from behind the straw. He held out the cat with a half-smile, and Sammi stepped closer to retrieve the animal.

"Thank you." She gathered Dicey in her arms.

An awkward silence filled the barn room. Dr. Wyatt stared at her. Sammi averted her eyes and gazed at the dirt floor.

"Didn't I see you yesterday at the grocery store?"

Shoot. "Um. Yes. I think."

"I thought so. I'm new in town."

Sammi nodded, averting her gaze. "And I'll come back when it's more convenient," she offered quietly and turned to leave. *So much for taking chances.*

The veterinarian laid a soft hand on her forearm. Sammi froze and stared at his fingers. "You're here now. There's no reason I can't check your animal. Follow me."

He lifted Dicey from her arms and within seconds, he and

her cat were gone, disappearing through another open door. Sammi bit her lip. She had no choice but to follow.

Maybe taking a chance was on her agenda today, after all.

CALEB HAD IMMEDIATELY RECOGNIZED THE WOMAN. It wasn't her voice, although he now remembered her desperate call from the night before. It was the woman from the grocery store a couple of days ago—the one who had caught his eye. The one who had sporadically and without warning crept into his head intermittently since then.

She'd checked out in front of him. *A half gallon of milk, a soft drink, three cans of cat food, and some other stuff....*

He recalled the timid way she'd glanced at him. How her long, slender fingers had grasped the change from the checkout clerk. The way she had lifted her gaze to look at him with those big, puppy-dog brown eyes as he crossed in front of her Chevy. More than once, her soft and innocent profile had slipped into his mind.

He wouldn't call her a stunning beauty, yet her quiet quality and wholesome good looks attracted him right away. Never drawn to flashy women, he found this woman was anything but—but he certainly liked her looks. Her eyes sparkled, and he wondered if she knew it. Their gazes had skittered off each other a few times in that brief encounter, and it was the one thing that he'd taken with him as they'd parted ways—the innocent and intriguing energy in her eyes.

He'd wondered if he would run into her again. After all, Harbor Falls was a small mountain town where everyone knew everyone else. Or so it had seemed to him. It was one appeal of moving to a close-knit community like Harbor Falls.

The likelihood that he would run into her again was high.

He hadn't expected it to be this morning, though.

Caleb ambled on into the clinic, in the main part of the barn. He knew she strolled along behind him, uncertain, he sensed. She appeared shy and a little timid. They walked through the waiting room and into one of his two examination rooms. Placing a calming hand on the quivering cat's back, he scratched behind the feline's ears. Lifting his gaze to the woman's face, he registered the hesitation in those still twinkling eyes.

The woman held a quiet beauty that had appealed to him days before. And still did now.

"I think she's rid of the hairball," she said tentatively.

Caleb glanced at the cat in his arms. Turning back to his charge, he set the white animal with black spots on the table, leaving a steadying hand on her back. "There, there now, pussycat. You're going to be just fine," he crooned, then glanced up. "Name?"

"Uh, Dicey. Her name is Dicey."

"No, I mean yours."

Her eyes widened. "Oh. Sammi Jamieson."

Caleb extended his free hand. "Caleb Wyatt. Nice to meet you." He offered her a grin. She smiled shyly, then glanced away, but her hand stayed within his for a few seconds longer. Slim, soft fingers lay in his. He took notice of her ragged nails and wondered if she had a habit of biting them. Once again, he sought her eyes, but when she didn't glance up, he quickly dropped her hand and turned to the cat.

"How long did you say you've had her?"

Sammi moved closer to the table and scratched under Dicey's chin. "Oh, about a month. She's a rescue, I guess. She came to my house. I fed her and she stayed. I guess I've given her a *furever* home."

"*Furever?*"

"You know, like *forever* but *furever*, because, well, fur."

He chuckled. "I get it."

"Anyway, I guess I've adopted her."

"Or she's adopted you."

Sammi's eyes met his. "Perhaps."

"Cats usually choose their owners with care." Caleb ran his hands over the animal, giving her a quick once-over, checked her ears for mites, and looked in her mouth. "I'd like to give her all her shots—rabies, feline leukemia, and so on—then check her for worms and such."

"Oh," Sammi answered, "that would be fine."

He picked up the feline and looked into its eyes. "Cats are splendid companions."

"I've never had one before."

"You'll get attached to her pretty quickly."

"I already have."

"Especially if you live alone."

"I know." She paused. "I do."

Caleb waited a moment before setting the cat down, looking into Sammi's face. "You live alone?"

After a moment, Sammi answered, "Yes. I do."

Satisfied he'd gotten the answer he wanted, Caleb turned toward the door leading to the back of the clinic and grinned. This was a switch. He hadn't grinned about a woman in quite some time. He had business to take care of.

He glanced back with what he hoped was a serious look on his face and this time, met her gaze full on. She held it. "If you'll wait here with Dicey, I'll be back in a minute with what I need to finish the examination."

She nodded, and he left.

As he gathered his supplies, Caleb realized he was smiling again. It was a welcome change.

Chapter Two

Dicey had fleas. Sammi was glad there wasn't anything seriously wrong with the cat. She reached out to take her from Dr. Wyatt's arms.

He made some recommendations about the type of food to buy for the cat, then handed her something for the fleas, a tube of hairball remedy, and instructions for both their use. "If you'll step out here, Miss Jamieson, then we'll settle up."

She nodded. "Of course, Dr. Wyatt." She risked a peek into his eyes. Hazel. She hadn't taken the time to notice before. She reached for her cat, and he placed the fur ball into her arms. His hand lingered a bit on Dicey's back, stroking. "That would be fine."

She followed him out of the examination room.

The clinic was obviously not set up yet for business. The room used as the waiting area and office was recently partitioned off from the main barn—she could tell from the smell of fresh paint and the pile of two-by-fours and sheet rock in the corner—as were the two examination rooms. So maybe that's why there wasn't a sign. Dr. Caleb Wyatt was just now setting up his practice? New in town?

One or the other. And since everyone knew everyone else in Harbor Falls, she suspected the latter. Dr. Caleb Wyatt *was* new in town.

She watched him slip behind a counter and start shuffling through some papers on the desk. He turned and grimaced, then shuffled some more. Sammi stood with Dicey in her arms and waited.

Dr. Wyatt rifled through more papers to his right. Then left.

Sammi peered behind the counter at the messy desk.

"Is there a problem?"

He glanced up. "Oh, no. Just give me a second."

She mentally clicked off the equipment haphazardly placed around the small office cubicle—a new computer, an adding machine, a phone and answering system, a state-of-the-art printer/fax/copier/scanner combo, and two four-drawer filing cabinets. Reams of paper and a small bookshelf overflowing with manuals and loose papers sat beside them.

Dr. Wyatt looked up again. "I'll tell you what. This one's on the house."

Sammi took in his puzzled expression. "Oh, no. I couldn't do that."

"No. I insist."

"Oh, no. I've been a total inconvenience." She was embarrassed.

He scratched his head and glanced about at the mess. "Look, I'm just getting this office organized. I haven't taken on many regular patients. Just a few I've run into in the neighborhood, or like in your case, an emergency."

"I don't think Dicey's hairball was an emergency."

"It was if you didn't know what was happening."

"I woke you and everything. Let me pay you something. At least for the medication." She reached into her purse and pulled out a twenty-dollar bill. *Sammi Jamieson does the right thing. Always.* "Here."

He looked at her but didn't move. "No. I insist."

The look on his face said he wanted her gone. He didn't care whether she paid him for his time or not. Sammi felt her face flame. "Oh, well then. Thank you."

A little humiliated at that thought, she turned with Dicey in her arms and headed for the door. Something queasy roiled up in her stomach. This always happened around men. She would say something wrong and, most of the time, didn't even realize what she had said. She assumed too much or the wrong things, and it turned men off. Obviously, he'd dismissed her so abruptly. What was it? Insulted his pride when she insisted on paying?

Hell. Of course. Damned foolish pride. *Will I ever learn?*

She'd taken only a few steps when he caught up with her. "Miss Jamieson, wait."

Sammi halted and looked at him standing to her left. He continued, "I'm not trying to run you off. This..." He glanced back to the office area, "this is a little embarrassing. I've been so busy the past few weeks trying to get the clinic ready, I haven't taken the time to organize the office. I couldn't find the proper paperwork. I haven't even had it printed yet. I didn't want to appear inept, so I just decided not to charge you for this visit. I hope you understand, and that when you need additional care for Dicey, you'll bring her back."

Sammi took a breath. She wasn't sure she'd heard a word he said. She was too busy watching his lips move. What had gotten into her? He wasn't ticked off?

She took a long look at his makeshift office. "Looks like you need some help."

Stepping back, he raked a hand through his hair. "You could say that again. Know anyone looking for a part-time job?"

Sammi shook her head and turned away. *Know anyone looking for a part-time job?* Um, well, no. She moved through the door to the outside, looking at the ground as she headed for her car. Suddenly she felt uncomfortable again, out of her element. "Try Harbor Falls High," she called out over her shoulder. "They may know of some business students looking for summer work."

"That's a good idea."

He was following her. She stepped quicker toward the car. "Talk to Caroline Jones. She's the business teacher."

"I'll do that."

"I'm sure they'll know how to operate your new equipment."

"Do *you* know anything about computers?"

She hesitated and slanted a glance at him. "A little."

"I'm a computer klutz."

"What you have there is pretty user-friendly." She'd noticed the PC on the desk and a laptop cocked open on top of a filing cabinet.

"That's what I've heard."

Sammi stopped beside her car and studied him for a moment. He'd kept pace alongside her until they reached the car. All she really wanted to do was go home, but she had the distinct feeling he was trying to hold her there with conversation. That startled her. "Well, I guess I'll be going now. And don't worry, I'll bring Dicey back."

She glanced at the door handle and reached for it.

"You wouldn't be interested, would you?"

Interested? Her head whipped back to look at him. "Excuse me?"

"The job."

"Me?" A hand went to her chest. "Oh, no. I have a job."

"Do you work nights?"

"No, I— Actually, I'm off for the summer."

"Oh, you're a teacher."

She shook her head. "No. I'm—" *Sigh.* "I'm an administrative assistant at one of the schools." Her voice lowered.

A slow grin spread across Dr. Wyatt's face. Sammi wasn't sure she liked it.

"Administrative assistant?"

Her chin dipped in a nod. "Yes. Kind of like a secretary, but we are moving toward using the newer terminology now... Actually, I'm the Administrative Office Manager based out of the elementary school."

He stared her in the eye. "Office manager. Hm. And you're off for the summer?"

She slowly nodded again. *Where is this going?*

"Do you know how to handle that equipment in there?"

"Um, yes, most likely." Dicey squirmed in her arms. She opened the car door and slipped inside, depositing the cat on the passenger seat. She shut her car door behind her, and Dr. Wyatt rapped on her window.

Huh?

She stared at him for several seconds, wondering how she was going to get out of this conversation. He stood his ground. It would be rude if she just drove off, wouldn't it?

Sammi rolled down the window. He leaned in.

"Then how about if I hire you for the summer?" he asked. "Just to help me get organized. Look, I don't know many people around here yet, and I don't have time to do a formal job search. I just need someone to organize the office and take care of some of this paperwork. Maybe get the computer files set up, if you can do that sort of thing, too. I really could use someone who knows what they're doing."

Alarm shot through Sammi. Work for him during the summer? This new guy in town? "I don't know... I'm not sure I want to give up my summer. I have plans...." Heck, what plans did she have other than reduce her to-be-read pile of books and piddle with her flower garden?

"Can you do spreadsheets?"

"Of course."

"Excel?" He paused, staring off. "Write letters? Memos? Invoices?"

"Well, sure, but...."

"Can you do a little accounting, too? Basic stuff. I have the software."

"Probably. I don't know about...."

"You're perfect. I'll pay you the going rate. No, wait. I'll pay you above the going rate. Actually, I'll pay you whatever you say *your* going rate is. Name your price. When can you start?"

Excuse me? Dr. Caleb Wyatt was pushy!

Still, she was tempted. A summer job would keep her busy. And the money would be nice. But it really wasn't about the money. Was it?

Of course, a little extra income wouldn't hurt—but something else made his suggestion so tempting. *Remember*, a voice inside her cried. *You want to change your low-key, boring lifestyle. Take some chances. Act a little more impulsively. You want to spice up your ordinary mundane lifestyle and risk something new. This is it! This is your chance!*

And she *had* been saving money to take a cruise. It was on her bucket list, and she'd been planning it for a while. It was the one thing she had promised herself she would do—force herself to do if she must—to take a chance and do something different. Spice up things. Something of her own. She had decided that taking a cruise was safe. It was self-contained, and there would be lots of activities and people.

Probably just the thing to help her feel a little more worldly. Not to mention getting her out of this mountain town for a little while. So yes, the money would be nice. She might book that cruise for Christmas break now.

Besides all of that, when would the opportunity come knocking again to work side-by-side with such an interesting and okay, handsome and appealing man? Not at Harbor Falls Elementary.

Go for it.

Sammi took a deep breath and looked long into Dr. Wyatt's eyes. She felt daring. This was her chance. She was going to do it.

Her stomach suddenly felt twisty at the thought. *No.* She shook her head. "Start? No, I'm sorry. I can't work for you, Dr. Wyatt. Good day."

With that, she started the car, and he stepped away. Good thing, because she gunned the engine a little too fast and left a little gravel spray behind as she left.

About five miles down the road, her heart stopped racing.

Stupid, stupid, stupid woman!

Sammi gripped the steering wheel and called herself every unpleasant name she could think of, and six ways to Sunday. Why couldn't she do it? She wanted to work for Caleb Wyatt this summer. And she'd wanted to say something cute like, "Sure, I'll help you get your office up and running, and is there anything else I can get *up* and *running*?" She'd always wanted to be the woman who would bat her eyelids repeatedly after a come-on like that.

She groaned. *You'll never be that kind of woman, Sammi.*

"You're an idiot, Sammi Jamieson." Pulling into her driveway a few minutes later, she parked and let her head fall against the steering wheel. "A total—complete—idiot." She tapped her head three times on the top of the wheel. "If you'd said something like that, Dr. Caleb Wyatt would have escorted you out of there so fast your head would spin. He's only interested in your secretarial skills—excuse me, office management skills."

But it could have been a nice, summer-long opportunity to get to know him better—and a pleasant divergence from her regular boring summer routine.

Dicey crawled into her lap. Sammi reached down and scratched behind the cat's ears, then lifted her head, resigned that her life would never change. She'd lived this way for too long. And it was her choice. "C'mon, you ball of fluff. Let's go do the laundry."

And laundry, she did. With every simple article she tossed into the washer, dried, folded, and put away, she browbeat herself until she felt like she'd gone through the wringer, body and soul, as well as pinned every one of her insecurities out on the line to fully inspect, pick apart, and worry over.

It was true. *I am insecure.*

She'd been told often enough by teachers and friends. It came from years of trying to be insignificant, unseen and out of the way. Then, as she grew older, from trying not to compete with her mother.

And of course, she was plain, not pretty. She'd heard that often enough, too. Especially by her mother—who was, of course, beautiful.

Sammi was dowdy. How she hated that word. Dowdy. Now, at thirty-two, according to her mother, she would soon be an old maid. *Old maid!* Did anyone even say that anymore? Probably not, but what would it matter? An old maid she would be. She'd live in this little cottage for the rest of her life and small children would run by and taunt her until she was in the grave because she was a dowdy, insecure, plain, old maid, crotchety spinster.

She was on the shelf.

Good gracious, Sammi! Get a grip.

If you put yourself on the darn shelf, then that's exactly what will happen.

Caleb Wyatt had probably already taken pity on her.

He probably already knew about her withdrawn ways. There were no secrets in Harbor Falls, North Carolina. Everyone knew she was a loner.

He probably even knew about her mother.

A flash of embarrassment crawled up Sammi's cheeks. She could never face that man again. She'd have to find Dicey another veterinarian.

———

IT WAS UNUSUAL FOR CALEB TO STAY UP LATE. Normally he was so exhausted from working on the clinic, repairing the barn, feeding the livestock, and trying to get everything to start up the practice, that he fell unconscious as soon as his head hit the pillow.

But tonight was different.

Tonight, he couldn't get the shy but charming Sammi Jamieson out of his mind.

He found her charming. There was something haunting and delicate about her looks and her mannerisms. Something he couldn't quite put his finger on. The way her gaze skittered past his when they spoke and the way she moved away from his touch made him curious. Who was Sammi Jamieson? And why was he thinking about her so much?

She reminded him of a frightened doe—with her huge brown eyes, cream-colored skin, and honey-brown hair—always with a timid expression on her face. A look of bewilderment, of questions never asked or answered.

He felt a bit in awe of her. Why, he wasn't sure. There was just something.

He shook himself and punched his pillow. Goober, his

black Lab, rolled over onto his back and deposited his head next to Caleb's on the pillow. The dog was soon snoring, mouth open, a little drool sliding out of the corner.

Caleb sighed, turned over, and closed his eyes. Between the dog and his ever-returning thoughts of Sammi Jamieson, he wondered if he'd get even a wink of sleep the entire night.

THE MOST AWFUL COMMOTION SAMMI EVER HEARD came from her kitchen. She bolted upright in her bed and then sat perfectly still with her sheet pulled up to her chin, listening. It was an unmistakable howl—a horrid, ear-splitting, otherworldly wail.

And it wasn't in her kitchen anymore. It was coming down her hallway.

"My God," she gasped. "What on earth...?"

Dicey lurked in the room. Sammi saw the glaring reflection of her eyes, then the silhouette of the cat's body as she stalked closer to the bed, her head turning one way, then another, in agitation.

"Meee-Owwww."

Sammi thought she looked like a miniature lioness on the prowl.

"Oh, my. You poor dear." Leaping out of the bed, Sammi bent to scoop up the cat.

"Rrrrrrr!" Dicey spat, swatting at Sammi's fingers as they curled around the cat's belly.

Stunned, Sammi jumped back and studied her kitty in the moonlit room. "Oh! What's wrong, pussycat? Your tummy hurt?"

Dicey stalked out of the room again. Sammi followed her through the house.

The wailing continued. Low, menacing, primitive. Then

she heard an equally primal answer from outside her kitchen window.

Dicey flew to the screened window, which Sammi had left open. It was still early summer, and she'd always waited until the last possible minute to turn on the air-conditioner—especially at night.

The wailing grew louder.

Dicey paced back and forth on the windowsill.

Out of the dark, a flash of yellow attached itself to the window screen from the outside, rattling it. The caterwauling escalated. Dicey became frantic, howling back, batting at the screen. Sammi put her hands over her ears.

"Dicey! What are you doing?"

The cat pawed. The animal on the other side screeched.

Sammi flew to her back door, broom in hand. The instant she pushed open the screen door, she flipped on the light. A huge yellow tomcat had attached itself, claw-by-claw, to her kitchen window screen.

"Oh, my!"

Sammi tried to approach the cat, which turned, hissed, and swatted at her.

Sammi whacked at the intruding demon with the broom.

Inside the kitchen, Dicey jumped down from the window. A second later, a slap of fur-flesh hit Sammi's back door, and a streak of white high-tailed it into the darkness. A blur of yellow followed.

IT WAS TOO EARLY TO GET UP, ACCORDING TO HIS alarm, so obviously the ringing in his head wasn't coming from the clock. Caleb squinted at the red numbers. Four-twenty-three. In the morning. Who? Who in the hell...?

If he didn't know any better, he'd say his practice was up

and running. Ready or not. Office manager or no office manager.

He huffed out a sigh. "Hullo?"

"Dr. Wyatt?"

"Hmmmm."

"Sorry to bother you." The voice was urgent. "Again."

"Hmmmmm. What can I do for you?"

"It's...my cat."

Caleb attempted to cover his yawn. "Yes?"

The person on the other end of the line sucked in a huge sob. He immediately became more alert. "Ma'am?"

"Oh, Dr. Wyatt. It's... It's just awful. She was making this horrible racket— I think she had a stomachache. And then she ran out of the house, and a huge yellow boy cat chased her. I kept hearing them screeching and howling and fighting, and I knew that strange cat was hurting my poor Dicey! And I couldn't find her, and then it was three hours later, and I heard her meowing from up inside the huge oak tree in my backyard, and now... Well, now I can't get her down and I'm afraid she's hurt." The caller took a deep breath, sucked in another sob, and sniffled.

Caleb closed his eyes.

"I'm so sorry to bother you. Oh goodness. I'm a mess. Poor Dicey."

Dicey?

His eyes shot back open. "Sammi? Uh... Miss Jamieson? Is that you?"

She exhaled and sniffed. "Oh, my gosh. I'm sorry. I didn't even tell you who I was. I didn't know what to do. I'm sorry I've bothered—"

Caleb cleared his throat. "Miss Jamieson, calm down. If you tell me where you live, I'll come by and see what I can do."

"Oh no. I couldn't."

"Yes, you can. Give me your address."

Chapter Three

"There, there, girl. You're going to be fine."

Grateful for his help, Sammi took the cat from Dr. Wyatt's arms, pulled her close, and then curled into a wicker chair on her back porch. Dicey lay exhausted in her arms, limp as an overcooked noodle. Sammi stroked her back and quickly inspected her pet, who seemed to enjoy the attention. After a minute, Sammi looked up. "She's okay?"

"She's fine."

Sammi hugged the cat. It had taken until daylight to coax her out of the tree, an open can of tuna providing an irresistible enticement. Dicey had gently picked her way through the branches and into Dr. Wyatt's hands. By that time, though, the cat was exhausted and an easy catch.

Dr. Wyatt took a few minutes to look her over and pronounced her fine. He sat across from Sammi now on the back porch.

"What do you think is wrong with her?"

"There's nothing wrong with her, Miss Jamieson."

Sammi looked him in the eye. "Oh, no, there was definitely something wrong. She moaned and groaned and whined, and when that other cat came to the window, she didn't like it at all."

He cleared his throat. "Miss Jamieson, Dicey is in heat."

Sammi let her mouth go slack. How could she have been so dumb? "In heat?"

"Yes."

"You mean she…?"

"Was feeling romantic. Very romantic."

"And the other cat was…?"

"Definitely interested," he said with a grin.

"And do you think they…?"

"I most certainly do, Miss Jamieson."

Sammi's cheeks grew hot. Dr. Wyatt hadn't taken his eyes off her face. "Oh."

"I'd look for kittens in a couple of months."

"Oh, goodness. Kittens?"

"That's usually what happens."

"I know that, Dr. Wyatt."

Sammi took in the hint of amusement that twinkled in his eyes. A few silent seconds passed between them.

"If she has a litter, then you need to consider having her spayed afterwards. And if she doesn't, you'll probably want to do that anyway."

Sammi nodded. "Okay, Dr. Wyatt. I guess that would be best."

"Call me Caleb."

Surprised, Sammi replied, "I just assumed that… I mean in your professional capacity—"

"Never mind that. Please call me Caleb."

Relenting, Sammi nodded, searching his hazel eyes. This man didn't look or act as if he were patronizing her. Maybe she was wrong. Maybe he didn't know about her. A shiver raced down her spine. "I'm Sammi. Miss Jamieson sits behind a desk in the school office." Sammi flushed at her words.

Caleb chuckled. Had she said something cute? Sammi risked a smile.

"Is there anything I can do to convince you to sit behind my desk for a while this summer? I really could use someone who knows what they're doing."

Sammi lifted Dicey firmly into her arms, her gaze glancing off his face. He looked and sounded sincere. Perhaps he really was interested in having her work for him. Her heart rate sped up in alarm. She hugged the cat, as if using her for some sort of protection, a shield. From what, she wasn't sure.

How many times does a girl get a second chance? The voice inside her screamed. *You blew it yesterday. Don't blow it today!*

"Well," she began, "I've been thinking that perhaps... I might."

The broad, amiable smile that spread across Caleb's face warmed Sammi's insides.

———

CALEB WAS GLAD HE AND SAMMI HAD WAITED UNTIL the next day to get started on the office. Neither of them had slept much the night before anyway, and he'd wanted to spend a couple of hours in the office making notes and getting things in order before she came, so he'd be able to tell her what was on his list. He hated leaving such a mess for her on day one.

But it hadn't worked out that way. The distress call came from the farm down the road. The farmer had tried for hours to pull a calf that didn't want to be pulled, and in the end, they lost the calf and nearly lost the cow.

Exhausted, his own chores waited for him at home, and he got right to them. He'd not stepped one foot into his veterinary office. Yet.

He expected Sammi at any moment, and he was a nervous

mess. The state of his office closely paralleled his state of mind, it seemed—and he was anxious about seeing her again.

Whenever she was around, she emitted some sort of calming aura. That's the only way he could describe it. Her gentle handling of her cat impressed him. She swore the tuna tempted the cat out of the tree, but he could say just as vehemently that the soothing nature of Sammi's voice brought the frightened feline down to safety.

There were moments when he'd thought he was going to have to climb the tree to get the animal down, but that wasn't necessary.

As they'd sat on her back porch, the sun just slipping up over the eastern sky, he'd observed her softness, her dew-eyed expressions, and her fresh innocence as she'd cooed to the cat. She was like a morning glory, unfolding and flowering before him.

Such a welcome change.

For six months prior to moving to North Carolina, his life had been nothing but turmoil and aggravation. When he'd finally escaped Montana and found this farm outside of the perfect small town nestled in these North Carolina mountains, he'd hoped he had found the peace and solace he'd craved. Prayed for, in fact.

He had no desire to dredge up the past, no need to think about the trouble in Montana, ever again. As far as he was concerned, Montana was ancient history.

SAMMI PUSHED AT THE BARN DOOR. SHE THOUGHT about knocking, but that didn't seem necessary at this point. Besides, she was showing up to work, and walking right on in seemed appropriate enough.

The door silently swung open, and she slipped inside the

clinic headquarters. Caleb, his back to her, stood scratching his head while surveying the chaos of his office.

"Looks like I got here in the nick of time."

Caleb swirled. She'd caught him off guard.

"Sammi. I didn't hear you come in."

"I rarely sneak up on people. The door was ajar."

He glanced back at the mess. "I don't think you've come a moment too soon. I apologize. I had intended to get in here and do a little organizing, but it didn't work out that way."

Sammi stepped into the room and glanced over the counter to the inner office. Then she looked up to meet his eyes. He stood about two feet away. "That's what you hired me for, wasn't it?"

A slow grin broke across his face. "It was. But this is embarrassing."

Sammi shrugged. It didn't look that bad to her. "I've seen worse."

"Really?"

"Yes. You should have seen the school office when I took it over. We'd just moved into a new building. The assistant before me, who had just retired after thirty years, knew nothing about technology or modern office organization, and didn't care to. Of course, she had her systems—they just weren't systems that anyone else understood. The place was a wreck. This doesn't look so bad."

"Do you think you can whip it into shape before you go back to work?"

Sammi swallowed. She didn't start back to work until mid-August. It was now early June. She could get this place whipped into shape long before then. She nodded. "No problem."

"Great."

Caleb walked to the back of the room, where a door led into the examination rooms. "So far, no more emergencies to handle today, so that's good. I haven't set up office hours yet, so there are no appointments. I'm going to feed and water my animals, then work on finishing out the examination rooms and the kennel out back. I've got a little more construction work to do on the back part of the barn. So, I guess I'll just leave you to whatever you need to do." He opened the door and hesitantly took a step through it, then turned back. "Do you have questions before I go?"

Sammi shook her head. She was eager to get started, and it was just as well that he would not be hovering over her shoulder. She worked better that way. Besides, him being around would make her extremely nervous. "You want me to do whatever I feel needs doing?"

He grinned, his eyes twinkling. "Exactly. It's your baby."

His smile broadened, and Sammi thought she was going to melt like butter on a hot biscuit. Geez, the man was something. And she was going to be working for him for the rest of the summer. Her mother wouldn't believe it.

Her mother had better stay far away from Dr. Caleb Wyatt.

"Okay. Guess I'll see you later."

"Guess I will."

He left and Sammi surveyed the office, which seemed suddenly empty with Caleb gone. She really didn't think it would take her that long to whip into shape—not as long as Caleb expected, anyway.

Unless she stretched things out.

No. Her efficiency and her work ethic wouldn't let her do that. When she was done, she was done. But from the looks of things, she had at least a couple of weeks of steady work ahead of her. Maybe three.

What will be, will be.

Hours later, Caleb pulled his flatbed truck next to the barn, expecting Sammi to be gone, but her car was still parked in the barn lot. Getting his practice up and running with clients would not be the issue. Having time to get everything done before the locals beat his door down *was* going to be the dilemma.

He'd had three calls that day. One before noon. He'd stuck his head in the office long enough to tell Sammi that he was going out and for her to take a lunch break whenever she felt like it. She'd poked her head up from behind the counter and waved him off without a word.

He'd no sooner patched up a calf caught in some loose barbed wire over at the Derickson place than he'd gotten another call on his cell phone about a stray dog hit by a car on the edge of town. Unfortunately, the dog had died before he got there, and a couple of men had already buried it. They talked him into a late cup of coffee at Sugar High Bakery, where he met the owner, Sydney Hart, who said she knew Sammi.

Small town, indeed.

He stayed a while, chatting and getting to know some of his new neighbors.

Harbor Falls was a friendly town. Slow-paced, easygoing people. He was going to like it here.

On the way back to his farm, he'd gotten another call from a man whose horse was refusing to eat or drink and hadn't for a day. He feared the horse was colicky, but when he examined the mare and talked to the farmer, he saw that a change in feed was the problem. The mare was just being stubborn and wanted her old feed back.

Now, as he got out of his truck, he wondered why Sammi hadn't gone home long before this. He pushed open the clinic door.

She greeted him with a smile. "Long day?"

"Busy. Didn't get hardly anything accomplished. How about you?"

She glanced shyly behind the counter. Caleb's gaze followed. Then he stepped closer to look over her day's work. Sammi followed behind.

He puckered his lips and drew out a long whistle.

The filing cabinets were now neatly lined up against the wall, and the stacks of files and papers lying about earlier had disappeared. The copier hummed in the background. The L-shaped desk was neat, clean, and organized—the computer up and running at one end. Fax machine, adding machine, and telephone were all precisely placed.

Caleb stepped further into the office.

A row of bookshelves, more than he had previously purchased, lined the back wall. His professional journals and books were organized according to subject. A bulletin board hugged one entire wall, tacks neatly pinned on one side. A dry-erase board hung above the phone for messages. She'd even tacked a couple of framed posters of dogs and cats on the walls.

A coffee maker, with a half-full pot of coffee, sat on a small cart in the corner. Cups, napkins, sugar, creamer, and sweet-ener lined the bottom shelf of the cart.

He turned to look at Sammi.

She glanced at him, questioning, then looked at the floor.

"Man, how did you do all this in one day?"

She timidly lifted her gaze to catch his eye and shrugged. "It wasn't much."

"It looks great!"

Her face brightened. "Really?"

"Yeah." He glanced again at the back wall. "But all this stuff wasn't here, was it?"

Sammi shook her head. "No. I hope you don't mind, but I ran into the local discount store and purchased a few things. I put them on an account at the store—I opened one for you. If you don't like that, I can take everything back, and you won't be out a dime. But you said it was my baby."

Caleb chuckled. "I did, didn't I?"

"Yes, you did."

"It looks great."

"Thank you. There's just a few more things I need to finish up tomorrow."

Something gripped Caleb deep in his belly. Tomorrow? He stepped closer to her. "You surely don't mean that you'll be finished tomorrow, do you?"

He watched Sammi bite her lip and glance away. "Well, I think I probably will be. Once I dug in, I realized there wasn't that much to do. It was mostly organization, Caleb. Things were a mess."

No. Too soon. Think, Caleb. Think. He'd been gone all day with no time to spend with her.

"So the computer is running?"

"Yes."

"And the files are in order."

"For what you have there."

"And I see you've organized my journals and books."

"It didn't take very long."

Damn. Now what was he going to do to keep her here the rest of the summer? "What about that accounting software program I bought? Did you figure it out?"

A frown crossed her face. "I haven't had a chance to look at it yet."

Yes! "Oh, well, then, I guess you'll have to stay a few days longer to figure it out. And I'll need some forms drawn up for my patients and accounting and payroll and billing and...."

Sammi put up her hand. "That will take me a little while. I didn't know you wanted me to do all that, too."

"Of course." Caleb breathed a sigh of relief.

He glanced around the waiting room.

"And this waiting room looks awfully dull. Don't you think?"

He watched Sammi's eyes scan the room. "It could use a little color."

"Yes, well, you must keep working," he said cheerfully. "I bet you know how to decorate. You can do that, can't you? I have no clue what to do."

Her eyes met his again, and Caleb felt swallowed in the deep brown depths of them. Then she smiled. "I suppose I could."

Caleb sighed again. "Good. Then you'll stick around a bit longer?"

She exhaled and glanced about. "Of course, Caleb."

That was a relief. If he had to think of things for her to do, he would do it. He needed time to convince Miss Sammi Jamieson that she might want to stick around a lot longer than summer.

He paused, watching her as she turned back to the desk and fiddled with some papers. Who was he kidding? He needed time to figure out if he was *ready* for her to be here longer than summer.

Chapter Four

Two extra boxes of file folders, two reams of paper, and a box of ballpoint pens teetered in Sammi's arms as she attempted to flip the latch to the clinic door. She clamped her chin onto the top of the box of pens and reached for the door handle. Slowly, carefully, she lowered to make contact with the metal lever until finally, still balancing her purchases between forearm and chin, she opened the door to slip inside.

Honestly, she didn't know how Caleb had managed so long without supplies. It didn't seem to matter how many times she went back to the store, she'd return to the clinic and realize there was something she didn't have.

Breathing a sigh of relief, Sammi straightened after she entered the clinic, gave the door a kick to close it, returned her free hand to steady the load of items on her arm, and turned to head for her desk.

Something large and black blocked her path. She saw it out of the corner of her eye first then it lunged.

"Rrrrrruuummmmffff."

Sammi dropped everything, flattened herself against the clinic wall, and screamed.

"Rrrrrruuummmmffff." The beast had two eyes, and it was slobbering, tongue hanging out. It set two huge paws on either of her shoulders, then licked her face.

"Ooooh, yuck!" Sammi frantically wiped the slime from her cheek.

"Rrrrrruuummmmmffff," it replied.

Sammi shrieked again.

The back clinic door burst open.

"Goober!" Caleb shouted. "Dammit!"

The dog pushed off Sammi and wagged his tail as he made his way to his master.

Sammi's right hand went to her chest to still her frantic heart, then she finally exhaled, shakily, but an exhale all the same.

"What *was* that thing?" she blurted out.

"It's only Goober." Caleb smiled, then immediately frowned and rushed forward. "Did he hurt you?"

"Goober?"

She watched his face break into a grin again. "His name is Goober. He's ridiculously friendly. Typical black Lab personality. He's my dog, and he wouldn't consciously hurt a flea. Don't you remember him from the first day you came here?"

"No." She exhaled again. "What about unconsciously?" She allowed herself a timid grin.

Sammi had a faint recollection of that day. There was a bawling calf, a squawking chicken, and Dicey scrambling out of her arms... Yes, there was a barking dog. A big, black, barking dog.

"Yes, I remember him. And no, I'm not hurt—he startled me, that's all."

Caleb stepped closer, mere inches away. Too close. She took a deep breath and a half step in reverse.

"I'm sorry. I don't know how he got in here. He usually stays in the barn with me. I guess he sneaked in here earlier to take a nap in the air-conditioning." He glanced down at the lump of black fur now making a mound at his feet. "Darned lazy animal anyway."

"He seemed rather energetic a second or two ago."

Caleb lovingly prodded the unmoving dog with his foot, then grinned and lifted his gaze to peer into Sammi's eyes. "Maybe. But Goober's a faithful friend. Been with me a long time. I promise you he won't hurt you. He's gentle as a lamb."

Sammi swallowed and tried to take in some more air. She nodded, then looked at the dog. "I admit he looks harmless right now. But I don't mind telling you, he scared the bejee-bers out of me a minute ago."

Nothing but silence fell between them for several lengthy minutes until finally Sammi mustered up enough courage to look up into Caleb's face. He stood watching her. Staring back at her. Much like that day at the grocery store. Heat crept up her neck, then skipped to her cheeks.

She couldn't help it. She had to look away.

Stepping backward, she tripped clumsily over a box of file folders. Caleb caught her arm.

"Whoa! Be careful there. Here, let me get this stuff." He reached for the files.

Sammi bent to pick up the box of pens. Her fingers felt like lead. "No, I'll get—"

She conked heads with Caleb as she went down.

Pain ripped through her skull. "Ow! Sorry!" Immediately, they both jerked upright, rubbing the tops of their heads. The box of pens slid from Sammi's hands and fell to the floor. Five hundred black, medium-point writing instruments scattered. Goober barely batted an eye.

"Oh, my gosh!"

She dropped to her knees and began gathering up the

pens, calling herself every kind of synonym for clumsy. Caleb Wyatt must think her an absolute klutz.

The top of her head was throbbing. His, too, likely.

"Sammi."

She started again, and a handful of pens jumped from her fingers, tossing about like pickup sticks.

"Sammi." The voice was close, but she ignored it, concentrating instead on depositing the pens carefully back into the box, one at a time. Sometimes two. The sooner out of this mess, the better.

Oh, God. How embarrassing.

"Sammi."

Gee... Would he just move? He was standing on a whole bunch of those blasted pens!

"Sammi!" Two large hands reached out and stopped her hands from darting hither and yon. "Sammi, stop!"

She did.

"Look at me."

After a minute, she did that, too.

"What are you doing?"

She gulped. What did it look like she was doing, having a picnic? She opted to forgo the sarcasm.

"I'm picking up the pens."

"Let me."

"Why?"

"Just let me, okay?"

"But I can get them, Caleb."

"I will do it."

"I repeat. Why?"

His lips curved into that sexy grin again. Sammi had a hard time keeping her eyes off his lips.

"Because you're dangerous."

"Wha—?" Sammi opened and shut her mouth three times

and couldn't get out the question. Dangerous? She? Plain Sammi Jamieson? The innocent little wallflower?

"I am not!"

"You are. And you're adorable."

She was certain shock raced over her face. "Ador... I am not!"

"Yes, you're adorable. And you're too darned dangerous for your own good. Or maybe for my good, I'm not sure yet." He was laughing. Smiling at her. Enjoying this!

"Wha—?"

Puzzled and flustered to no end, Sammi had no choice but to let it go. She sat back on her heels and let Caleb pick up the rest of the stuff. Then she rose and made her way to the desk. He followed in a couple of minutes and stacked the items in front of her.

"I can take over from here." She avoided looking at him.

He stood beside her for a long moment. "I'll be in the barn," he said, then left. Chuckling.

"I suppose I'm amusing, too," she said under her breath. She glanced back at the closed door where Caleb had just exited.

I'm adorable?

Right.

IT WASN'T OFTEN THAT CALEB FOUND HIMSELF amused at someone else's expense but amused he was. "Yes, Miss Jamieson, you amuse me very much." Amusing. Adorable. Dangerous. All three. Miss Sammi Jamieson was all that. And he liked it.

She was dangerously close to melting his heart. Dangerously close to pushing him over the edge. And dangerously close to being perfectly and irresistibly lovable. That soft smile, that nervous twitch of a grin, those huge brown doe-eyes were just...dangerous.

The kinds of things that made a man glad he was a man.

It was difficult to keep out of the clinic, to push thoughts of Sammi out of his mind, and difficult to concentrate on the tasks at hand, but he forced himself. Caleb knew beyond any doubt, that he wanted Miss Sammi Jamieson in his clinic, his barn, for a long time.

His life?

But she was skittish as a startled horse, and he'd have to be patient.

—————

THE NEXT MORNING, SAMMI COULDN'T HELP BUT smile to herself. An evil thought passed through her mind. She looked again at the list on the computer screen.

Yes, these things would keep her busy for quite some time.

She smiled again.

Since yesterday, she'd known she was going to have to come up with a plan. So, being the organized and efficient administrative assistant that she was, she'd made a list. Periodically, she'd added to that list, which just kept growing.

Sammi had even made a special file for it on the computer. She didn't want to name the file something obvious, because she didn't know if Caleb ever used the computer after she'd left for the day. She didn't want him to suspect she was dragging out her summer job responsibilities. So, she'd pondered and thought about it and come up with a naming convention that he would likely pass over and not give the time of day. Finally, she named the file STDL, for *Sammi's To Do List.*

The thing was, she didn't want to wind up this job any sooner than she had to. Caleb was her employer, and she didn't want to exploit him or anything. She wanted only to be paid for her honest work. She had finally admitted to herself, however, that she wasn't in any hurry to leave this summer job.

So she kept adding to the STDL.

She loved organizing things. She enjoyed playing around with the new software program on his computer. She wanted to be around the animals.

And well, Caleb Wyatt, too.

Even though every time he came near her, she literally tingled, and found herself edging away, not wanting him *too* close. Of course, she didn't want him to think that she liked him—liked him a lot. Because if he thought that, she figured she'd be out of there fast, real fast.

She was there to work for him. He wasn't interested in her in any other way, she was quite certain. She'd decided that late last night. At first, she'd thought there was some sort of sexual implication in his words. She was *almost* flattered. Adorable? She must have been hearing things. Dangerous? Phooey.

He simply meant what he'd said. She was dangerous. Period. And that's why she had to convince him otherwise. She had to convince him she wasn't a klutz. She had to convince him she really was the efficient, organized office manager he'd hired.

But she also didn't want to be too efficient. She wanted to stay around for as long as possible.

That's why she'd made that list of legitimate tasks. And if she'd made herself one slightly evil little promise about the list, it was this one: just don't work *too* fast, Sammi. Stay busy, but don't get all the jobs on your list done too quickly.

The door swung open from the barn, and Sammi quickly closed the file. Her spine tingled as footsteps approached from behind.

"Sammi, are you busy?"

She swiveled in her desk chair to look at Caleb.

Skin bronzed by the sun, hair disheveled as always, but it

was a sexy sort of disheveled. And his hazel eyes, which sometimes looked golden—if she let herself investigate them deep enough—always made her hold her breath a little longer than normal.

"Did you need something, Dr. Wyatt?"

He grinned. Lord, she was a goner.

"Sammi, please call me Caleb."

He'd continually reminded her of that the past three days.

She nodded. "Sorry. I forget. It's my training," she offered.

"Forget your training." He smiled again. "I'm not all that big on formalities. From now on I'm Caleb, and you're Sammi. Okay?"

Sammi felt her cheeks getting hot. She nodded again, then glanced away. "Okay."

"Good!" He stepped closer. "Now, I was wondering if you could help me with something."

Sammi stood. "I can try."

"I just need another pair of hands."

"Oh, okay."

"Just to steady something while I hammer."

She stepped closer. His grin became wider. Some sort of tension shot straight down into her belly. "I... I think I can do that."

"Okay, follow me." He turned and Sammi finally exhaled, then followed him out into the barn. Darn it! She glanced at her hands. They were shaking so badly she didn't know if she could hold one stupid thing while he hammered.

And speaking of hammering, her heart was doing a decent job of that. She needed to get a grip.

CALEB PICKED UP HIS HAMMER AND SHOVED THE handle into the loop on his tool belt. He felt a little guilty. He really didn't need any help here. It was just that for the entire morning, since Sammi had arrived exactly at eight, he'd been thinking of ways to get her into the barn, or of excuses for him to be in the office.

Well, he thought he'd give this a shot, anyway. He had too much work to do himself to justify sitting around watching her work all morning. Yet, that was exactly what he wanted to do. And exactly what he *wouldn't* do. Hell, he'd scare her off for sure then. No, for every moment of getting close to Sammi that he could manage, he was going to have to come up with a legitimate reason. Otherwise, she'd hightail herself out of his clinic and his life so fast his head would spin like a child's top.

He bent to pick up the edge of the six-by-eight piece of wall he had just framed for a storage closet. "Sammi, if you could help steady this, it would be a big help." He glanced her way. She was just behind him. "Wait until I get it upright."

Within a few seconds, he had righted the framing and had slid it next to the wall. "Okay, can you come over here?"

Sammi moved closer to him and reached for the two-by-fours.

"Here?" she asked. "Like this?"

A hint of strawberry wafted past his nose. Her shampoo? Likely. Sighing, his knees weakened.

"Caleb?"

"Oh, yes. Right here." He moved to his left and showed her how to steady it. Sammi leaned slightly into the framing and looked up. He stared straight down into her eyes. "Yes, like that, that's just fine."

Yes indeed. This is fine. Caleb could have stayed lost in her gaze all afternoon.

"This is getting...awkward."

Caleb jumped back. "Right."

He re-positioned the framing and started nailing into the studded barn wall. "Just let me get this first, then I'll have to brace it until I'm ready for the other wall to go in." He hammered some more. "Are you okay back there?" He glanced over his shoulder.

"Yes."

"Okay."

Caleb quickly finished. "Now let me get another couple of two-by-fours to brace this with." He looked at her again. "Are you sure you have it? Don't let go yet."

She nodded.

He started for the pile of lumber but looked back at her once more. Her hair was down. Why hadn't he noticed that this morning? Usually she pulled it back, but today she'd let it loose, framing her face. And were those freckles across her nose? Why hadn't he noticed them before?

"You've done something different with your freckles."

Sammi's eyes grew wide. "Excuse me?"

"Your freckles...you've done something different."

"My freckles?" One hand flew to her nose.

Caleb shook his head. "No, I mean your hair. You've done something different with your hair. I like it."

Sammi touched a tendril at the side of her face, blushing.

"I just let it down."

The framing shifted.

Sammi yelped and tried to push it back.

Caleb paled as the two-by-four framing fell, and he rushed forward to grab the wall at the same time as Sammi. In his haste, however, he overdid his effort, and the framing teetered forward, then backward, as they tried to steady it.

Sammi frantically clutched at air and wood.

Caleb pulled her back and out of the way as the framing crashed and splintered. Sammi shouted, and Caleb's heart jumped to his throat.

After a moment of deafening quiet, he braced both hands

on her shoulders and turned her toward him. "Are you okay?" He gave her a quick once-over.

Sammi nodded quickly. "I'm fine."

"Are you sure?"

"Yes, I'm fine, Caleb. It fell the opposite direction."

"I know, but you yelled."

"Oh... I think I—" She glanced down at her hands, turning them palm upward. There was a scrape between her thumb and forefinger on her right hand and a small line of blood. "I guess I might have a scratch or something. Maybe a splinter."

Caleb took her hand in his and looked into her eyes. Hell! Why did he do this? His obsession with Sammi had gone and gotten her hurt! He would never forgive himself. Taking a deep breath, he tried to calm his pounding heart.

"Sammi, I'm sorry. I shouldn't have had you out here helping me."

"It's just a scratch, Caleb. I'll be fine."

He rubbed his fingers over the back of her hand. "Damned straight you will. Come with me."

He didn't give her one second to protest. As he led Sammi away from the office and through the clinic door, he called himself every word for stupid he could think of, every step of the way.

"No need to make a fuss. It's only a splinter."

The look Caleb tossed her then almost made Sammi want to shudder. It was a worried look, a look of utter concern. It was the look every woman wanted to see from a man.

Protective. Caring. Taking control.

And that worried her even more.

Before she knew it, she was sitting on the edge of the sink in an examining room, looking at the first aid paraphernalia scattered about: cotton balls, peroxide, rubbing alcohol, bandages, a package of needles, tweezers, and a washcloth.

He'd already gently cleansed her wound, concentrating closely on what he was doing, carefully washing away the blood so he could examine it.

He glanced back down at her palm. She followed his intense gaze. It *was* a splinter, and it was quite a big one. It had ripped her palm open right in the space between her thumb and forefinger.

Caleb tugged.

"Ow."

He glanced up. "Sorry."

"It's okay, just get it out."

"I'm trying."

Sammi noticed his hands were shaking. Maybe she couldn't trust him with the tweezers. "Maybe I should get it out myself."

"No, I'll do it."

"But your hands are shaking."

Sammi watched him take a steady breath and try to calm himself. Why was he so upset? It was just a scratch and a splinter, no big deal.

"Don't you perform surgery on animals?" Sammi queried.

Caleb slipped her a sideways glance. "Yes. Of course."

"Do your hands always shake like that when you do?" Sammi couldn't believe she'd said that and hoped he didn't think she was being sarcastic.

Caleb straightened, closed his eyes, and took a deeper breath. As Sammi watched his shoulders finally relax, his eyes opened, and he looked her square in the face.

"You're not making this any easier, you know."

Sammi swallowed. Hard. "I—I'm not doing anything."

"Yes, you are."

She didn't know what he meant.

"I don't—"

He shook his head. "Never mind. Now, just sit still and let

me do this, okay?" His voice had softened and had lost a bit of its edginess.

"All right."

Sammi did as he asked. Something was wrong with Caleb. Something about the way he was acting unnerved her. He had to be angry with her. He'd asked her to help him, and she'd gone and done a stupid thing, letting go of the piece of framing. Oh geez. He's mad at me for messing things up, putting him behind schedule. Breaking the wall. Now he'll want to get rid of me for sure.

He tugged again. "Ow!"

"Got it."

"Good."

Caleb looked up and grinned widely. Suddenly, his nervousness eased. "I'm sorry I hurt you."

She shook her head. "You didn't."

She watched as he soaked another cotton ball in the antiseptic, cleaned the wound again, and covered it with some sterile gauze.

Sammi took a deep breath to steady herself. "I'm sorry I messed up back there." Then she stared at the wall behind Caleb.

"What?"

"I messed up. I'm sorry. I let go." She mentally traced the pattern made in the paneled wall as she recalled the vision of the framed piece falling over. "I'm so clumsy at stuff like that. I'll understand if you want to fire me."

She couldn't look at him. She just couldn't. He was going to get rid of her; she knew it. Closing her eyes, she turned her head further away from Caleb.

The gentle touch of his fingertips under her chin startled her. The warmth, more than anything, made her finally look up. She jerked, and Caleb gripped her chin firmer, then tilted her head until her gaze met his and held.

"Sammi, I don't want to fire you."

She gulped. "You don't?"

Caleb grinned that irresistible grin of his. "No, I don't."

"But it was my fault."

"No. It was mine. I shouldn't have asked you to help me in the first place."

"But—"

"Don't argue. It was my fault." Then he glanced back once more at her palm. Sammi watched as he carefully and gently finished bandaging her wound. He cut the gauze to size, then taped it securely. When he was finished, he held her hand a little longer than necessary, and after another few seconds, Sammi watched as he began gently brushing his fingertips across her palm.

The sensation skittered up her arm and crossed over her heart.

She risked looking at him. He was frowning and staring at the pattern he was making there, and the look on his face made her heart beat faster. It was a look she wasn't sure she'd ever seen on a man. At least not any man who was looking at her.

Then Caleb did something almost unbelievable.

He lifted her palm to his lips and placed a gentle kiss right there in the center.

Her heart did things in her chest that Sammi had never experienced.

Had never felt.

Flittered. Sizzled. Beat hard against her ribs until she was breathless.

Oh, damn.

Chapter Five

"So where have you been keeping yourself the past few days, Sammi? I haven't seen you at any of your usual haunts. You know, the library, Ralph's, the bakery."

Sammi took a sip of her tea and mentally bit her tongue. She would *not* argue with her mother today. *Today*, she was lighter than air.

Today, she was in the best mood of her life.

Today, Caleb had kissed her palm.

She sighed and recalled the flustered look on his face immediately after he'd done it. She wasn't sure which of them had been more surprised. After that, everything was a blur. She had muttered something about getting back to work. He had mumbled something about her taking the rest of the day off. And both had scurried off, uttering things neither of them had heard or understood.

Sammi went back to her office area and left him a note saying that she might as well do as he said and that she would be back early in the morning. Once she'd gotten home, however, she was just too restless and decided she needed to get out of the house. Why she ended up at her mother's, she hadn't a clue. But here she was.

"You didn't answer my question, dear."

Distracted, Sammi gave her mother a smile. "I've been working."

A penciled eyebrow arched.

Her mother was beautiful, had always been beautiful. Unfortunately, she was also the town tart, and everyone in Harbor Falls knew that too and accepted it.

Everyone but Sammi.

Women, watch your husbands!

How difficult it had been growing up knowing that she was the plain child of a beautiful woman. The kind of woman who caught flies with honey, batted her fake lashes, and oozed sweet tea and Southern euphemisms until they both soured with a slice of bad lemon and hurt feelings.

Her mother had shot down every attempt she made to pretty herself up. Finally, Sammi had just given up and accepted her fate. She would never be as lovely as Desiree Jamieson. She would never possess that kind of beauty.

Never be homecoming queen. Never be the county fair princess. Never be runner-up for Miss North Carolina. Nor did she want to be.

Yet, all those accolades somehow went to her mother's head and had turned those good looks into something else over the years.

After her father died, her mother turned to any man who would give her the attention she craved. How embarrassing it was as a young teenage girl to discover your mother chased every available man in town, and quite a few who weren't? Sammi never asked her mother about it, nor had she cared to know the details. Sammie knew she would choose a different lifestyle for herself—one that was in every way the opposite of her mother's.

"Working?"

Sammi sipped more tea. "Yes, Mother."

"I thought you were finished for the school year."

"I am." She was deliberately vague.

The brow arched higher. "Have a cookie, Sammi. They're low carb."

Sammi watched her mother's perfectly manicured hand push the plate of cookies on the coffee table toward her. Queasiness gripped her stomach. "No thank you, Mother."

"One won't hurt you."

Sammi shook her head. "The tea is just fine."

Why is she pushing the stupid cookie? Usually, she's chiding me for wanting a cookie. At least lately.

The plate clattered against the coffee table. Sammi registered the agitation. She attempted to ignore the anxiety, which had knotted itself in her stomach. Every cookie she had ever eaten reminded her of the summer between her years in junior high. The summer when Sammi's mother had decided Sammi was not eating enough, was getting too skinny, in fact, and had urged cookies and ice cream on her all summer long. If Sammi hadn't known better, she would have thought she was trying to fatten her up.

"You have a summer job?"

Sammi mentally debated what her answer should be. She had to be careful. Things were unstable at the clinic. Not with Caleb's business, but with her relationship with Caleb. She'd been trying to figure that out all afternoon. When she'd taken the job, she knew Caleb only wanted her there for her organizational skills. But now?

Now she knew only one thing—she couldn't let Caleb know she was interested in him. No, that was impossible. If he suspected she was interested in being more than his office manager, he would fire her for good. She was sure of it. And even if that weren't the case, it was not in her makeup to throw herself at him like a... Like, well, like her mother.

No, that wasn't her style.

"Sammi? You have another job?"

Giving up her introspection, Sammi sighed. "Yes. Yes, mother. A part-time one."

"Do you need money?"

"No."

And yet, even though she wouldn't act on what happened earlier today, she still wasn't sure what the kiss on the palm meant. It could have been a simple gesture of sympathy for her wound, or an impulsive act, or something he'd thought about doing all this time.

She was obsessed with trying to figure Caleb out.

"Sammi, did you hear me?"

She glanced at her mother. "Oh, sorry. Did you say something?" She investigated her mother's face and saw her mouth moving with words apparently coming out of her lips, but her brain was still back in the barn with Caleb, thinking about how his mouth lowered to her hand and that sweet brush of his lips over her palm.

"Pookie is feeling a little under the weather. I think I may need to see about him."

The gesture was the one that confused her. Could Caleb be interested in her in more ways than for her work? And if so, why?

"Sammi!"

Her entire body jerked. "What!"

"You're so preoccupied. I don't understand why you came by to visit if you will not talk to me."

Oh, were you talking to *me mother? I thought you were talking* at *me.*

"You've barely said a word and have sipped at that tea like

it's the last you're ever going to get. You didn't even make a comment when I told you about Pookie."

At that moment, the ancient Pekinese jumped onto Desiree's lap for effect. *That dog gets more attention than I ever did.*

"Sorry. Is Pookie ill?" Sammi refocused. After all, she was here. *Give Mama some time before she interferes in places you don't want her, Sammi.*

"Just not himself lately. I think he can't poop."

Good Lord. "Maybe he should eat some grass."

"Oh, that's ridiculous. Now, you tell me why you're here and tell me about this job."

There. There it is. The inquisition.

Sammi registered the emphasis her mother had put on the word *job*. Her mother hadn't worked in the years since her father died. He'd left her with a nice little home and a fat insurance check, which she'd promptly invested in all the right places. Now, she was sitting pretty. There was money held in trust for Sammi, too, because Desiree had certainly taken advantage of her situation and had played her cards well.

"I felt like working."

"Why on earth?"

Sammi shrugged. "I needed something to do."

"And what are you doing? Typing resumes for some secretarial service? Oh Sammi, if you're going to insist on working, why don't you take some of your money and go back to school to get another job, make a career for yourself, something other than that flunky secretary job at the school."

"Administrative assistant."

"What?"

"I like my job, Mother. And we don't use the term secretary anymore."

Desiree rolled her eyes. "I know you like it, sweetheart. But really, you could do so much more."

"It's an important job. People rely on me."

But her mother really didn't hear what she said. She stared instead, and Sammi expected her next words. "On second thought, dear, perhaps you're right. Maybe you *have* found your little niche, and you're quite happy where you are, so you should just stay. I'm not sure you could handle anything more challenging anyway."

There it was. The putdown.

It always came at some point in the conversation. A brief, "Sammi why don't you," invariably followed by, "But of course you wouldn't be interested in that, or couldn't handle that, or finish that, or be good at that..." Her mother's digs changed little.

It was the reason Sammi never quite felt she had any self-esteem to speak of. Having been shot down and belittled repeatedly, it had been difficult for her to pick herself back up.

Sammi rose. "Thank you for the tea. I'm tired. I'll be going home now."

"But darling, you haven't—"

Sammi put up her hand. "Another time. I really must go—"

She let herself out of her mother's house before she could get up enough courage to say exactly what was on her mind.

———

LATER THAT AFTERNOON, SAMMI CURLED UP IN THE recliner in her family room with Dicey on her lap. The cat yawned lazily, gave Sammi a heavy-lidded look and settled, happily purring, into the nest she'd made for herself.

Gently, Sammi stroked the top of the cat's head, noticing the look of pure bliss on the animal's face. Dicey was the picture of utter contentment. That made her smile.

What was it Caleb had said? That a cat chooses its owner

or something to that effect? Well, she was certainly glad that Miss Dicey had come along. The cat was a welcome addition to her life.

Never had Sammi taken care of an animal, and she had let nothing living ever depend on her as Dicey did.

Oh, she knew the cat could probably fend for herself. She'd probably gotten along well enough as a stray. But now she and Sammi had each other. And it was nice.

For many years, Sammi had thought that she needed nothing or anyone to make her life complete. Now she knew she had been wrong.

Would she ever feel the contentment that Dicey felt?

She frowned.

Sammi stopped stroking the cat's head and studied the pixie face of the sleeping animal. Yes, she supposed it was possible. If a woman found the right man, she could be a lot more than content. And for the first time in her life, Sammi wondered if she'd found that man. Or, as in the case of Dicey, if the right man had found her.

THE SMELL OF FRESH COFFEE GREETED CALEB AS HE entered the clinic. He took one sniff and stopped in his tracks, closed his eyes, and inhaled long enough to absorb as much of the welcome aroma as he could.

He was out of coffee at the house. And he'd slept late. Thankfully, Sammi had already started a pot. He could kiss her.

Whoa. No. Not yet.

Caffeine. Yes. That's what he needed, and plenty of it. Not kisses, well...of course that would be nice, but... But caffeine would have to be the thing to get his blood pumping this morning.

His night had been restless. As were the two nights prior. Since it had become common knowledge that the new guy in town was starting up a veterinary clinic, something had interrupted his every night's sleep.

Except lately, his lack of sleep stemmed from things other than work. Last night he'd had more on his mind. Correction. Just one thing, er person, keeping him awake.

Sammi.

God, he had kissed her hand! He had brushed his lips across the delicate skin of her palm and had savored every sensation his lips had felt at the touch.

He had to be crazy to rush her like that.

Why had he done it? It had scared him to think that she might run away and never come back because of what he'd done. Caleb had paced the floor most of the evening and into the night. And then, after finally falling asleep, he'd slept through the alarm. After a quick shower, he'd headed straight for the clinic, half-afraid to find that Sammi had quit.

But there she was, Miss Efficiency herself, sitting at her computer, the coffee maker gurgling in the background. Just like normal.

Normal? And what was normal anyway?

Was this his new normal?

He *could* get used to it.

The door slammed shut behind him, and Sammi jumped. Pivoting at the sound, her eyes grew wide, and her hand went to her chest.

"Oh, my goodness!"

A smile crept across Caleb's face. Not because he'd scared her, but because of how innocent and beautiful she looked sitting there looking back at him.

He glanced at the door. "Sorry. I guess I should fix that thing."

She shook her head. "It's okay. You just startled me." She

turned back to the computer. "I am working on these patient forms. Guess I was hyper-focused."

He wished she'd turn around and hyper-focus on him. He suspected she'd turned away, so she didn't *have* to look at him. If she would only make eye contact with him for longer than thirty seconds, he'd be happy.

Slow, easy steps, he told himself. One little baby step at a time. Convincing Sammi of how much he was attracted to her, of how beautiful she was to him, was going to be a process he'd enjoy. But he must remember to move slowly. The lovely lady was as shy as she was sweet.

"Mind if I have a cup of coffee?"

She glanced over her right shoulder. "Don't be silly," she said in an uncharacteristically sassy tone. "It's your coffee, you know," she added.

He grinned. "Yes, I suppose you're right." But Caleb just stood and watched her slim fingers glide over the keyboard. They were long and delicate, with oval nails slickly polished to a clear sheen.

He stepped slowly toward the coffeemaker as his gaze moved past her fingers and wrists, up her lightly freckled arms, then further past her shoulders to the delicate arch of her neck.

Abruptly, Caleb turned away. He had to rein in quickly the notions playing through his mind. But try as he might, he couldn't. They just kept coming back. And the one—the one that did him in more than anything—was the image of him sweeping back the thick brown hair at the nape and placing one kiss after another up and down its warm ivory length.

Easy, boy.

Caleb picked up a coffee cup.

And dropped it.

"Damn," he muttered. His hands were shaking.

"What?"

Scooping up the wayward item, he straightened his body. "Nothing. Just dropped the thing."

He glimpsed briefly into her eyes before she turned back to the computer. After another moment, he slowly reached for the coffeepot and poured a mug full.

"Want some?" He glanced her way.

Her fingers stilled, and she turned in his direction. After taking a deep breath, she raised her head and looked him full in the face.

She held the gaze for perhaps ten seconds.

Caleb didn't want to breathe, afraid to move one iota.

"Yes, I think I will," she answered. "I'm ready for a break."

Caleb told himself to get a grip.

He poured her a cup of coffee. "Black?"

"No," she answered. "Artificial chemical sweetener, please. I love the stuff." She rose, unaccustomed to having anyone wait on her. "I know it's bad for you, but...."

She didn't finish the sentence. He motioned for her to sit down. "Sit still. I've got it." In the next few seconds, he scooped up a couple of little blue packets, a plastic spoon, and both mugs and headed for the L-shaped desk. He sat Sammi's coffee beside her computer, deposited the sweetener packets and spoon there as well, and then took a seat in the chair next to hers.

The room was quiet for a moment while Sammi opened the packet of sweetener and tapped it delicately into her cup as Caleb watched. How was it possible that such a simple, everyday act like that could be so, well, sexy? Every little thing she did charmed him.

Sammi stirred her coffee, lifted the cup to her lips, and glanced over at Caleb. Quickly, she cradled the cup in her hands on the desk and glanced at her lap.

"Please not do that, Caleb?"

She'd taken him by surprise. "Don't do what?"

"Look at me."

"Oh. I'm sorry. But why not?" He teased.

"Because it makes me uncomfortable." She still stared into her lap.

Caleb studied her for a moment. "The last thing I want to do is make you feel uncomfortable, Sammi, and I'm sorry if I did. I won't stare at you."

She lifted her gaze, her eyes darting. "Thank you. I'm just weird like that. You know, with the staring thing."

"Well, of course." His grin relaxed into a frown. "Again, I didn't mean to make you uncomfortable, even though it shouldn't."

"But it does."

Caleb took a deep breath and moved his chair a little closer. "Sammi, look at me."

She was hesitant, but he didn't have to ask a second time. Slowly, she met his gaze. Caleb savored every second.

"You're a beautiful woman. I like to look at you."

She closed her eyes and glanced away. Touching her chin, he gently nudged her gaze back toward his. "I mean that sincerely."

It was at that point that Caleb realized something was wrong. Something more than just Sammi's shyness was a factor here. It was difficult to understand the range of emotions crossing her face. Fear, panic, uncertainty, disbelief —he wasn't sure which showed the most, but they were definitely all there.

And that's when he knew he had his work cut out for him.

Sammi Jamieson was one shy and reserved, yet tough cookie to crumble. But oh, when that day came, he would savor every single crumb.

Chapter Six

"I don't see any reason you can't come to work with me, do you?"

Dicey purred, content where she was, as though she truly understood what Sammi had said. If she hadn't known better, Sammi would have thought her cat grinned.

She scooped the spotted feline into her arms and stepped toward her back door. "Really, you could stay in the office with me all day long today while I'm finishing up those patient forms and keep me company, couldn't you?"

Dicey yawned wide, showing her pointy teeth. Sammi took the animal's indifferent yawn as a sign of acceptance.

"Okay. Since you agree, then I'll gather up a few things, and we'll be off."

Sammi sat the cat down on the table, then placed a can of cat food, a baggie of dry nibbles, and an old plastic butter bowl for Dicey's water into the sack containing her own lunch. Glancing about the kitchen, she scrunched up her lips, wondering if that was all she needed to bring. It could be a long day. Caleb had mentioned the day before that he might be gone when she got there this morning and not be home until late that night because he had to drive into Johnson City for some supplies.

Oh, litter. She had one of those disposable pans she'd bought at the store when she thought Dicey would not be here long. She'd take that, too. That way Dicey wouldn't get lost outside if she had to, well, go.

Satisfied that she needed nothing else, Sammi picked up the cat, the supplies, and headed for the door. One of these days she would get the silly cat carrier.

IT WAS PROBABLY THE MOST RIDICULOUS FORM OF payment he'd ever accepted for a job, but what was he to do? Caleb wasn't the guy to refuse treatment to an animal when its owner had told him right up front she had no money. The poor bird was in a terrible fix, and his owner was in a panic. Somehow, the scarlet lorikeet had got hold of a large sunflower seed, which had jammed itself sideways into his throat, preventing the bird from closing its beak. By the time Caleb had arrived, the poor creature was thrashing about, as the woman, who was of absolutely no help, sobbed hysterically next to the cage.

Caleb knew the bird would soon choke if he didn't intervene, so he gritted his teeth, opened the cage, and stuck his hand in.

To say he disliked birds was an understatement. Caleb disliked birds with a passion. Yes, he was an animal lover, but birds were a species he'd never quite allowed into that circle of affection. He couldn't let any animal suffer though, so he plunged ahead in the rescue attempt.

Oh, why hadn't he gotten away early this morning as he'd planned? Instead, he'd hung around to see if he could spend a few minutes with Sammi when she arrived at work, then was caught by the frantic call of the bird owner.

His red-feathered friend scratched his hand, and Caleb jerked back.

The woman sobbed loudly.

Caleb tried again, this time more quickly.

Not sure how he did it so fast, he snagged the lorikeet with his right hand, bring the creature closer to him, extract the wayward seed with a pair of tweezers he had readied for just that task, then hastily deposit the bird back into his cage.

He stood for a minute and watched the little scarlet demon.

The bird puffed out his chest and acted as though he were swallowing—once, twice, a third time.

The bird looked at Caleb, then at his owner, and finally said in a scratchy voice, "Hi, you S.O.B. My name is Petey. What's yours?"

It was then that the grateful owner took down the cage from its hook and handed the package, lock, stock, and bird-bath to Caleb. She wouldn't take no for an answer. She was that grateful to him for saving Petey's life.

Caleb suspected she was ready to rid herself of the nasty bird, anyway.

But what could a guy do in a situation like that? Caleb grinned sheepishly and accepted the gift.

SAMMI MENTALLY CHECKED OFF HOW FAR SHE'D gotten on her STDL. She was sure she'd crossed off all the office paraphernalia that needed purchasing, and she'd done all the office organization she could. Patient forms, billing and accounting forms, purchase orders and letterhead were all completed and ready for use. She'd taken the original documents to the printers early yesterday. Of course, this was only a small order, but enough to get them started. There would be more coming in another couple of weeks.

Nothing left to do in the office.

But she still hadn't tackled the waiting room. That was another reason for her trip into town that afternoon. She'd made a list of the essentials to purchase and another list of more decorative items for the room. Third, she'd made the rounds of area stores to gather prices so she could discuss with Caleb just how much "decorating" he wanted her to do.

Sammi slowly and carefully opened the clinic door. It had become a habit now, ever since Goober had made known his unexpected presence several days earlier. She was making headway with the dog, though, or perhaps she should say that the big ugly lug was making headway with her.

The coast was clear, so she stepped inside and deposited the boxes of forms on the table, then turned to retrieve the rest from her car.

"Oh!"

She ran smack-dab into Caleb. Immediately blushing, she jerked her hands back, where they had, of their own accord, landed palm down on his chest. She tried to step away but couldn't—her back was right up against the tabletop. Was it her imagination, or did Caleb take a half step closer?

"I thought you were busy all day?" she said breathlessly, then looked away, embarrassed. After a couple of seconds, she slowly met his gaze. Determined, she held that gaze for longer than her usual shy sideways glance. Besides, he had friendly eyes to look into, and maybe, just maybe, he enjoyed looking into hers, too.

It could happen, she told herself.

"I never got into the city," he told her. "I had an emergency call this morning, then I came back here and finished work on the kennel, and then I had lunch. What have you been up to this morning?"

"I'm just back from town. I picked up the forms at the printer."

He was looking at something behind her. Was he listening?

"And then I visited several stores to get some prices on things for the waiting room."

His eyes moved barely to the left. No, he didn't seem to listen.

"Then I ran into Godzilla at the gas station, and later I had coffee with Queen Latifah and Elton John at Sydney's bakery."

"Uh-huh," he replied. "That's good."

He wasn't listening.

Slowly, Sammi turned in the same direction as Caleb. At about the same time, he asked, "Sammi, what did you do with my bird?"

She jerked back to look at him again. "Bird?"

"The scarlet lorikeet."

"The scarlet what?"

"What did you do with Petey, my new bird?"

"I didn't know you had a new bird, Caleb."

This was weird.

He stepped behind the counter and led her to an empty birdcage sitting beside the computer, its little door slightly ajar.

She looked at him. "When did you put that there?"

"This morning."

Sammi gulped and frantically glanced about the room. It had to have been after she left to go to the printer. Oh, God.

"Did you come in after or before I left?"

He shook his head. "I don't know."

"Oh, my gosh."

Caleb fixed his gaze on her then. "Why?"

It was then they both heard the feeble squeak and turned toward the partially open door leading out into the barn and kennel. Dicey, her mouth full of red feathers, poked her head around the corner. Another faint squeak sounded.

"Dicey! What in the hell is she doing here?"

Sammi rushed toward the cat. "Oh, goodness, Dicey! Give me the bird!"

Sammi stuck out her hand. Dicey growled.

"Easy. She'll bolt."

"Oh God, Caleb. I'm so sorry!"

"We'll talk about it later."

Sammi bit her lip and nodded. She crouched to coax the bird-snatching Dicey a little closer. "C'mere babykins. Let Mommy have the birdie, okay?" She stretched out to rub a finger along Dicey's nose.

"Grmrrrrrrrr."

Sammi looked helplessly at Caleb.

"Here, let me. You will not baby-talk that cat out of a bird." He boldly reached forward, snagged the cat by the back of the neck and—

Goober bounded in the clinic door, took one look at Dicey and the bird, let out a tremendous volley of barks and lunged forward, all in one motion.

"GrrrrRRRRRRRRrrrrr!" Dicey clawed Caleb with her back legs, and he dropped her. The cat bolted into the barn, and Goober chased her, still barking. One red feather floated in their wake.

"Ah, hell."

———

ALL CALEB COULD THINK ABOUT WAS HOW HE hated birds and how that woman was so grateful to him for having saved Petey that she'd entrusted her precious pet to him, and now the damned thing was going to be lunch for a cat. He raced for the barn, then realized Sammi had already beaten him out the door.

Funny, he thought, if this had happened to someone else. A white cat with its jaws clamped around a little red bird being chased by a large black dog making enough noise to wake the dead, being chased by a woman with frantic eyes, being chased by a man who didn't give two hoots for his new red-feathered friend.

He felt guilty. Even though he didn't like the bird, he didn't want Dicey to eat it. What would he tell its former owner next time he saw her?

Guess he could always tell her Petey flew away. He didn't want to think about it.

The cat raced over hay bales, with the dog following close behind.

He watched Sammi leap the one, clamber over a second, and hike one leg up a little higher while stretching to reach the third stacked bale. They were like stairs leading up to the loft ladder.

Caleb stopped in his tracks and just watched. He knew exactly what was going to happen, and it did.

Dicey climbed the ladder, the bird still in her mouth. It only took her a few leaps and microseconds to get there.

Goober stopped cold at the base of the ladder and barked until the cat was out of sight. No way could that lug of a dog leap up into the loft from there. He wagged his tail and walked off, panting happily. His job was done. He'd scared a cat for the day.

Sammi, on the other hand, was still calling out Dicey's name as she climbed up, until she topped the ladder and fell over into the loose hay. He heard her call the cat again.

Caleb grinned.

As long as he lived, he'd remember this day, the way

Sammi ran free and uninhibited through his barn, her honey-brown strands of hair trailing behind her. He'd never forget watching her backside as she went leaping and bounding over hay bales as she climbed the loft ladder. He'd never forget how his insides turned to mush and his legs went weak just from the sheer pleasure of watching the woman he loved.

Loved.

Oh, hell.

She'd forgotten about her shyness.

She was just herself. Just Sammi. And oh, how he loved that.

Caleb joined in the chase.

Within a few seconds, he'd scaled the hay bales and the ladder and was in the loft. For a second, he stood, letting his eyes adjust to the dim light. He could hear Sammi but couldn't see her.

"Sammi?"

"Shh..." he heard. "I'm over here."

The voice came from his right. He glanced in that direction, then spied her.

Sammi had Dicey backed into a corner, the bird still clamped in her jaws. Sammi crouched, trying to entice the cat with a piece of wiggling straw. The trick wasn't working, and Dicey was eyeing her suspiciously.

He drifted closer until he crouched beside Sammi. "Why don't I take the left and you take the right? Then we both head toward the middle and hope that one of us can get ahold of her if she leaps."

A tiny squeak sounded from Dicey's mouth. "Oh, Caleb," Sammi said, "I'm so sorry about your bird. I didn't know...."

Her face said all she didn't say in those few words. She was genuinely sorry and concerned about the lorikeet. He put a hand on her arm. "It's okay, Sammi. Let's just rescue the bird, and then we'll talk about it, all right?"

She nodded and glanced again at Dicey. "I'll take the right."

He then stepped to the left and watched her move in the opposite direction. They both moved slowly. Dicey growled and watched them both warily. Caleb could swear the cat could see peripherally, not moving a muscle, her eyes taking in every movement they made.

Sammi took a step toward the cat.

Caleb took one too.

Sammi took another.

Then Caleb lunged at Dicey.

The cat howled and leaped, with the bird squawking feebly in her mouth.

Sammi jumped toward both cat and bird, but the bird fluttered away. Caleb leaped too.

Somehow, Sammi ended up on her back in the loose hay, with Caleb square on top of her, looking down into her lovely face.

The cat skittered off to safety somewhere, while the lorikeet, safe and sound, perched high above them in the rafters.

But neither of them thought much of the bird's safety.

Sammi's eyes were about as big, round, and brown as Caleb had ever seen them. Her flushed cheeks rivaled her moist pink lips. Her hair was all askew, with pieces of hay sticking out all over.

He smiled down at her.

Hesitantly, she smiled back. It was a quick smile, and then she licked her lips, and they straight-lined again.

Caleb picked away one piece of straw, then another. He didn't want to move. She felt so good underneath him. He liked looking down at her like this. He hoped it wasn't the last time he'd be able to do so.

"You've got straw in your hair," he whispered.

She raised a hand. "I do?"

He nodded, smiling. "Leave it, you look cute that way."

Her cheeks instantly pinked darker. "I'm not cute."

"Oh, yes, you are."

Her flush traveled to her neck, and looked even cuter.

God, how he wanted to kiss her.

Should he?

He probably should get up. But then, she wasn't asking him to, was she? And she seemed comfortable in the soft bed of sweet-smelling hay.

Oh yes, he wanted to kiss her. And he wanted to do more than that, but a kiss would be a reasonable place to start.

He risked tracing the outline of her upper lip with his forefinger. Sammi flinched, just a little, and he searched her eyes.

They didn't tell him to stop. In fact, she opened her mouth a little wider, and he traced her lower lip, too, letting his finger slide a little further inside. He could swear he felt her tongue lick his fingertip, just a little. He could swear he felt her tremble beneath him.

God, he wanted to know this woman. She'd put a spell on him from the beginning. And now, well, he was going to kiss her and get it over with, or he was going to have to exert extreme self-control.

Looking deep into her eyes again, Caleb mustered up his courage and dropped his gaze. Her tongue darted out, moistening her lower lip. He shifted closer, glanced quickly back up into her eyes, and saw that they were closing.

He kissed her.

His lips gently caressed the softness of hers—wet, sweet, and full of promise. He covered her mouth with his, and she responded almost as eagerly. Short, quick, hungry kisses, and then her lips stilled. He didn't dare go farther. Not yet. Not now. He pulled away and looked into her face again.

Her eyes were open. Her expression was puzzling. He couldn't quite read it, couldn't quite grasp what it meant.

"Caleb," she finally whispered. "Please let me up."

He swallowed, then obliged.

Sammi quickly rose off the hay and headed for the ladder. She didn't look back.

Caleb watched her go, realizing only one thing about what had just happened—he'd just experienced the sweetest kisses he'd ever had in his entire life.

And if he were a betting man, he'd bet Sammi had experienced the same thing, too.

Chapter Seven

It was all Sammi could do to keep from running as long and hard and fast and far away from Caleb as she could run. In fact, she nearly did just that—ran rather than walked hurriedly. Finally, she stopped right beside her car and made herself face what had just happened inside the barn.

He had kissed her, and he'd *wanted* to kiss her. She wasn't some charity case that just needed kissing. No, that wasn't the case—Caleb had *desired* her, had *wanted* to kiss her.

Her! Plain Sammi Jamieson.

Of course, she'd wanted to kiss him, too.

This changes everything, she told herself. Everything.

Didn't it?

She wasn't sure. All she knew was that she was confused, that her heart rate had escalated into the dangerously high range of about a trillion beats per second, that she was out of breath and her skin tingled all over and, most importantly, that she didn't want to leave.

She didn't want to run away.

Suddenly, she wanted to face this head-on, just to see where it all might lead.

Could she do it?

Sammi shook her head, unsure. She'd had nothing that could qualify as a romantic relationship for some time. All the good men her age in this mountain town were claimed and accounted for—and she'd always been too shy to do any of the taking. There was no one in Harbor Falls who interested her— at least, that's what she'd told herself. Something about having a boyfriend in her hometown turned her off. People talked.

And, well, there was all that gossip about her mother. Sammi knew the truth all too well. Would people think she was like her mother if she dated?

She'd never risked finding out what people might think.

Suddenly, she didn't care so much about what people thought.

But oh no... She couldn't leave right now, she thought, glancing toward the barn. She did not know where Dicey had gone, and she couldn't leave her here.

Sammi knew it was a feeble excuse for staying, and nowhere near the real reason she was turning back. Oh yes, she had to find her pet and probably should also help Caleb capture the bird, but the real reason was that she had to figure out how to go about capturing something else—her courage. But what if she ended up capturing Caleb Wyatt at the same time?

She trembled slightly at the thought.

But if she captured him, she wanted to keep him. She wasn't about to play games, and she wasn't about to be some-one's casual lover. And she hoped that was how Caleb felt. But she had to be sure.

CALEB STARED UP AT THE BIRD. HE HADN'T A CLUE what to do about Petey, who sat perched high above in the loft rafters. He could see the lorikeet's red chest rapidly vibrate as it expanded—as if Petey's little heart were trying to catch up after being scared too badly to move while in Dicey's mouth. Petey looked down, cocking his head one way, then the other, studying the vast expanse of barn surrounding him.

The bird squawked. "Hi, you S.O.B. My name is Petey. What's yours?"

Caleb grinned. At least he was alive.

He figured there was only one thing to do—leave the bird alone until he came down. There were other birds that lived in the barn. He supposed this one would be fine, as well. First things first. He had to find Dicey and get her out of the barn and back to Sammi. Second, he'd put Petey's cage in the barn somewhere, food and water inside, with the door propped open and hope the bird would eventually decide he preferred the comforts of home to the perils of the barn.

And third, he had to have a talk with his administrative assistant.

SAMMI OPENED THE BARN DOOR AND MET A FLUFFY white face. Caleb had caught her cat.

She grinned, sighed, and reached out for the animal. The cat snuggled in her arms. Looking up, she caught Caleb's amused expression.

"Thanks, Caleb," she said, embarrassed all over again.

"You're welcome."

"Did you find the bird?"

Caleb entered the clinic and shut the door tight behind him. He wiped his brow, then crossed the office and sat in Sammi's chair. "No, but he's in there, sitting pretty, up on a rafter. You know, if I were him, I wouldn't move either."

He grinned, and Sammi felt as if she were about to melt.

"Let's just keep the door shut so Dicey can't get in there. I'll take the cage in later and some food, and hope Petey will decide he prefers the smaller confines of the cage better than the barn's wide-open spaces. If not, well, then I guess we'll just leave him in the barn."

An awkward silence fell between them, and Sammi glanced at her toes. Dicey wriggled in her arms. "I'm sorry, Caleb. I guess I should have asked about bringing Dicey here today. But I thought you were busy all day, and I didn't think you would mind. She's good company."

He rose and stepped closer. "Sammi, look at me."

She did.

"I don't mind if Dicey is here. I don't mind at all. You did not know about the bird. In fact, when I left here this morning, I hadn't a clue I would come home with a bird. I don't even like birds."

"But—"

He silenced her with a forefinger on her lips. Sammi froze. She couldn't speak if she wanted to.

His eyes, oh my gosh, his eyes spoke so much they frightened her.

"Not another word," he whispered. "None of this is your fault. Maybe I'll explain it all later. Right now, there's something else that I need to do."

His finger was still on her lips, sliding back and forth, caressing her tender skin there. Caleb moved closer. Sammi felt something deep in her belly jump. Oh goodness, she *was* going to melt. Dicey squirmed. She was holding the cat much too tight, but she clutched the animal to her, anyway. Protection, perhaps?

Or, maybe it was to keep her arms occupied. To keep her from throwing her arms around Caleb's neck and making a damn fool out of herself in about two seconds flat!

His eyes again... Sammi couldn't look away. He held her

there, connected by a power she never knew existed. No way she was leaving now.

Caleb drew her closer, the cat still between them. Then gently, very softly, caressingly, he placed his lips on hers.

It was perhaps the most intimate, most loving moment she'd had in a long, long time. Maybe ever. Just a tender kiss, soft not rushed. She wanted to breathe deeply, take all the nuances of the kiss with her, deep inside of her, and keep them there. She wanted the act of kissing to go on forever. She wanted to feel like this, exactly like this, for the rest of her life.

Sammi barely registered the distant creak of the clinic door to her left. There was no way her brain could register anything other than the sensual warmth of Caleb's lips on hers.

No way, that is, until she heard the door abruptly shut and a familiar, irritating voice pierced the beautiful fog that surrounded both her and Caleb.

"Samantha Jamieson! I should have known you were keeping something from me. You've finally snagged yourself a man. How unbelievably cute. And just like you to go for the farmhand."

Mother.

Sammi could have died right there on the spot.

CALEB FINALLY REGISTERED THAT SOMEONE ELSE was in the room. Abruptly, the feeling that had enfolded them, just the two of them, shattered. And with that, Caleb felt Sammi's body grow rigid. Tense.

She quickly drew back.

Damn it.

For once, he felt he'd had all of her. With every fiber of his being, he'd held her in his embrace. Body. Soul. Heart. And she had given in. Her lips softened beneath his, and even though the cat was between them, he could feel her heart beating against his. This was the moment he'd waited for, the moment he knew he might make Sammi his.

Then that damn door creaked, and he'd lost her.

"Mother!"

Caleb turned toward the woman stepping into the clinic. *This* woman was Sammi's *mother*?

She was the epitome of sophistication. Not that he was impressed. The woman wore expensive designer clothes, he figured, although he couldn't swear to it—what did he know about designer clothing? Her hair was carefully styled, bleached blond, of course, and she wore jewelry. Lots of jewelry.

She was the type of woman most men would look at and immediately identify as "high maintenance." She did her best to look like she was rolling in money, but somehow Caleb doubted that. He wasn't sure why, but he did.

She spoke to Sammi, and he took in the smooth, Southern dialect that reeked of class and breeding. Or at least faked class and breeding. He figured it was the latter. For all her supposed sophistication, for all her affected charm, Caleb disliked her on the spot. The woman was a phony.

Or an also-ran.

Whatever.

Like, well... Like another woman he'd known once, not so long ago.

Immediately, he put that thought away as Sammi spoke.

"This is Caleb Wyatt, Mother. *Dr.* Caleb Wyatt, my employer. He's opening his new veterinary practice here in Harbor Falls. I—I'm just helping him out for the summer. Getting his office together, and, uh, stuff like that."

Sammi was talking much too fast, and Caleb could only guess it was because she was nervous, or hoping to get her mother the hell out of there. He hoped it was the latter. He shared her sentiment exactly. With each word Sammi spoke, she took a careful step backward, away from him.

He put out his hand. "Nice to meet you, Mrs.—"

The woman put up one palm and gestured while she placed the other in his. "Just Desiree. Desiree Jamieson. There hasn't been a Mr. in my life for quite some time. Thank God. So nice to meet you."

He shook her hand and abruptly let it go. She tried to hold on to him for a little longer. He peeled himself out of her grasp and thrust his hands into his pockets.

"How did you find my little Sammi?" She glanced at her daughter.

Sammi was obviously agitated. Caleb's gaze lingered over her for a moment. She fidgeted with Dicey's collar and nervously brushed her fingers through the cat's fur. Her eyes darted about and she appeared to be almost frantic. Something was wrong. He wished he knew what.

He forced himself to look back at Desiree. "She found me, Mrs.—Desiree."

He figured he'd humor her and call her by name. She arched an overly plucked brow at his statement, then turned to look once again at Sammi.

"Oh? My, aren't you full of surprises, Sammi? First, a summer job, and second, playing kissy face with the doctor." The smile she threw at her daughter's way was almost mean, Caleb thought. Damn her for making Sammi so nervous— and for interrupting them.

"Mother, why are you here?" Sammi tilted her chin, just a little, and looked the older woman square in the eyes. Caleb could tell it was taking a lot out of her, but she seemed determined.

"Why, darling, I'm sure you know. Dr. Eckle is getting quite old. I need to find someone new for Pookie—remember, I told you he was having difficulty going poopsie?—and I'd heard that Dr. Wyatt here was opening a new clinic just outside of town. So I came looking."

"Harrumph." Sammi rolled her eyes. *Poopsie, indeed.*

"Never expected to find you here, though, my dear. What a surprise. Tell me again how you got here...?"

"Mother, it's simple. I made an appointment with Dr. Wyatt for the cat. One thing led to another, and now I have this summer job. It's as simple as that."

Caleb noticed Sammi intentionally left out any reference to the "kissy face" comment.

Desiree beamed. "And one thing led to another? Hmm.... That seems obvious." She threw Caleb a challenging look. "Now don't you go breaking my daughter's heart, Dr. Wyatt."

"Mother!"

"I have no intention of doing that, Mrs. Jamieson." She just lost her first-name privilege.

Sammi huffed out an enormous sigh and blushed visibly, looked away from them both, and retreated a few steps. Caleb couldn't do anything to get her attention. All he wanted, all he cared about, was to make her understand he knew what was going on here, that he understood everything. He wasn't sure how, but he did.

Sammi's mother was dangerous. Not to him—he'd dealt with women like her before—but to Sammi. And he didn't like it.

He looked Desiree Jamieson straight in the eyes, and she stared right back. She had to know he didn't like her. Her eyes held a challenge. Desiree Jamieson was warning him away from Sammi. Why? He did not know.

"Sammi is about the most efficient person I know," he began. "She's really whipped this place into shape. You should have seen the mess it was in before she got here."

"I'm sure," she replied.

"I don't know what I would have done without her."

She smiled a broad, white-toothed smile and placed a hand on his forearm. "Oh, Dr. Wyatt, I'm sure you would have thought of something."

Once again, she stared him down, and Caleb didn't dare break the connection. "Well, I'm not so sure of that," he replied.

Finally, Desiree turned to her daughter. "Well, dear, I must be on my way. Lunch, you know, at the country club, with the garden ladies. I just wanted to see what had been keeping you so occupied lately. But now that I am here, could you make an appointment for my little Pookie? I am worried about his poopsies. Soon as possible, please? Just let me know when."

"Of course. I will do that."

She turned toward the door, then back again, staring at Caleb. "You know, come by the club sometime, Dr. Wyatt, for lunch or dinner. It's so much better than any place in downtown Harbor Falls."

"I actually like the places I've been to downtown. Amie's Place is rather nice."

"For breakfast, maybe." She tilted her head and grinned again. "Come now, *Caleb*. Someone of your stature in the community should have lunch at the club. You're a doctor, after all, and I'm sure you golf. Right. You'll want to join as soon as possible. I'll call you. Perhaps next week. And we'll arrange something."

His stomach roiled, and he could almost taste the bile. "Thank you, but no, Ms. Jamieson. I'm not one for 'the club' as you call it."

Desiree eyed him curiously. "Oh, I'm sure you'll change your mind about that, Caleb. Knowing the right people in this town matters. Think of the contacts you'll make. Business, you know."

"I don't think so. I'm doing fine with my local clientele."

"I can make sure you are properly introduced."

"I'm fine on my own. Thank you."

She held his gaze for another couple of seconds, almost as though she couldn't believe he would challenge her, then spun for the door. "It's been a pleasure, Caleb. Sammi, call me. We haven't talked in ages." And with that, Desiree Jamieson left.

"We had lunch just three days ago," Sammi whispered.

Caleb turned to her. After another second or two, Sammi let Dicey drop to the floor and collapsed into one of the mismatched chairs lining the wall. She exhaled, and then her face went into her hands. Her entire body shook once, then quaked and trembled.

Caleb sat beside her and waited. Finally, she stilled, took a couple of deep cleansing breaths, exhaled again, and looked up to stare at the opposite wall.

"I'm so embarrassed. And I'm sorry."

"You want to tell me what that was all about?" Caleb watched her profile. Everything about her face appeared long and sad. And there were tears. Just a glimmer, but they were there.

"Sammi?"

She shook her head. "Not now."

Caleb reached over and grasped her right hand. He took her long, slender fingers in his and softly caressed each, one by one. He cradled her hand in his palm and held it there for what seemed like a small eternity.

"I hate my mother," she finally said.

When Caleb looked back into her face, he knew she spoke the truth. The second Desiree Jamieson had entered the room, Sammi had turned into a different person. He just hoped he could get the old Sammi back.

"Do you want to talk about it?"

She gave her head a quick jerk. "No." She rose then, glancing at him only briefly. "No, I don't want to talk about it.

Not yet. Not now, maybe never. I don't know. Right now, I just want to go home. If that is okay with you?"

It wasn't, but what could he do?

He nodded. With no fanfare, she picked up Dicey and headed for the door.

Caleb let her go. He wondered if he'd just let her walk out of his life.

Chapter Eight

Three days later, Sammi sat on her back porch watching the sun slowly set over the Blue Ridge foothills on the horizon to the west. Her little frame house sat on the edge of town, a few miles from the lake, and down the road from Suzie Hart's Sweet Hart Inn, a local and popular bed-and-breakfast.

Miles of rolling hills stretched beyond her property. Just one thing she loved about living here.

Harbor Falls was a quiet place, small mountain town, rural America at its best, complete with its share of quirky characters. Like many other small towns, she supposed. Sammi figured she was right up there with them. How could she not be?

She had always been a little different.

Desiree had definitely been different.

All her classmates from elementary school had married years ago and had babies by now. Or they'd gone to college and settled elsewhere. Some simply moved away to make a name for themselves somewhere else. She'd barely dated in recent years. She actually enjoyed living alone on her little piece of land. Now, with Dicey as her primary companion.

She was content—most of the time.

Except for times like these, late in the evening, when the sunset was gorgeous, the air was warm, and the night birds were just calling. That was when she wished she had someone to share things with. Someone sitting on the porch swing with her, not speaking a word if they didn't want to. Just someone to *be* with.

She'd wanted no one before now. Not until Caleb, that is. And suddenly, she missed having someone around. Him.

The beep-beep-beep of her cell phone sounded from her open kitchen window, breaking the evening's silence, telling her she had voicemail. She'd turned the sound off on her phone two days ago. Dicey stirred on her lap, yawned once, then settled back in. Sammi waited for a few seconds, contemplated letting it go until later, then finally moved the cat to the side and slipped back into the house to retrieve the phone.

Two more voicemails. Not surprised. Yesterday, there were six.

She dialed voicemail.

"Sammi, please pick up next time. I need to talk to you. I just want to know that you're okay." Then, after a pause of several seconds, the phone clicked off again.

It had been like that for three days. She hadn't been back to the clinic. After the fiasco with her mother, she just couldn't face him. She'd played the scenario out in her mind repeatedly, and each time she'd become so humiliated and embarrassed that she couldn't stand to think about it.

Once again, her mother was ruling and attempting to ruin her life.

So, she'd checked out for a while.

She'd gone nowhere except her back porch for three days. The first day Caleb called once to check on her, he'd said. He asked her to call him, then had left her alone. Yesterday, he'd called half a dozen times. Today, well, it had been quite a lot more than that.

She could tell from his voice that she'd worried him. That bothered her a little. Heck, it bothered her a lot. She didn't want him to be upset, but she knew soon he would give up and move on. It's better like this, she told herself. Caleb doesn't need a woman like me. Besides my work there is finished, so there is really no reason to return.

At least, that's what she kept telling herself.

There was a second voicemail. She waited. "Sammi. Darling, call me. We need to talk."

Her mother.

Talk. Everyone wanted to talk. Desiree Jamieson was the last person on earth she wanted to talk to.

Sammi scooped up the plump cat and headed for her back door. In the kitchen, she plugged her phone back into the charger and made sure the sound was completely off. She poured some nighttime nibbles into Dicey's bowl, then after that, headed for her bedroom. Since there was nothing else to do, she might as well get some sleep.

If that were at all possible. She'd barely slept since the day Caleb kissed her.

———

CALEB HUNG UP THE PHONE.

He'd told himself repeatedly that he should just let her be. Leave Sammi alone to think about whatever had upset her so greatly and let her return to work when she felt like it.

But what if she didn't?

What if she never came back? He couldn't let her go, not like that. As if he didn't care about her.

Caleb glanced around the clinic and felt the icy silence of

the four walls surrounding him. He'd been so damn busy for days, even after Sammi had arrived. Now, when he would welcome something to do, he had nothing. He'd finished building the kennel yesterday morning. He had no calls, no appointments lined up.

Not even the Pookie appointment—Desiree had canceled —which had pleased him to no end. He had no desire to see that woman again.

Too much time on his hands and it was driving him nuts!

He'd even checked out the office, looking through the filing cabinets to see if anything needed organizing. He couldn't find anything. She had done it all and done it well.

Sammi Jamieson had breezed in, organized his life, and vanished.

Caleb raked a fistful of fingers through his hair and plopped down in Sammi's chair in front of the computer. He flipped the thing on. Maybe there was something here he could do. Hell, he could at least play solitaire or something.

This waiting was driving him crazy.

The machine ground to life with bings and clicks and flashes of screen and icons. Within a few minutes, he was clicking on this file and that, checking all that Sammi had done. He was impressed.

She'd started a database of the clients he had already served. She had inventoried almost everything in the clinic, it seemed, and of course had made forms for accounting and patients and such. He clicked on another file—STDL. Odd name for a file, he thought. It opened on the desktop monitor.

SAMMI'S TO DO LIST glared back at him from the top of the page. He scrolled down through the list. Most of the items had dates in the "finished" column, but there were a few at the bottom of the list with no dates.

Without hesitation, Caleb flipped the switch on the

printer and pushed the button at the top of the screen. The printer chortled to life and spat out the list.

Sammi Jamieson would not get off that easily. She still had work to do.

———

THERE WAS A POUNDING IN HER EARS, AND IT wouldn't go away.

At first, she thought it was part of her dream. She was in the clinic office, and Caleb was hammering in the barn, and....

The pounding continued. Sammi woke with a start.

Was it in her dream?

Dicey had moved from her favorite spot near Sammi's feet. Sammi stretched, and then she heard the pounding again.

Someone was at the front door.

Quickly, she put on her robe and hurried toward the front of the house. Dicey sat in the entryway looking up at the door.

"Who's there?" Sammi squeaked out.

"It's me, Sammi. Caleb. Please open the door?"

Sammi swallowed, then ran a hand through her hair. "What do you want, Caleb? I was sleeping." She didn't want to let him in, didn't want him to see her like this.

"I just want to talk to you, Sammi. You won't answer my phone calls."

What could she say? It was true. "I know."

"Why?"

"I don't want to talk right now."

"Please let me in, so we don't have to shout through the door?"

Sammi chewed her lip.

"Caleb, it's late. I'm tired. Can we talk another time?"

"When?"

Oh geez... Now he was going to pin her down. "Maybe next week?"

"No. I want to talk now."

"Caleb—"

"Please?"

Oh, God. Sammi stepped to the door and opened it a bit. She peered through the screen door, staring at his shirt more than anything else.

"May I come in?"

"Caleb, I—I'm not dressed." Immediately, her face flamed.

"Sammi, I don't care about that. I don't mind you wearing your robe. I just want to talk." His voice lowered, and Sammi liked its huskiness.

"Caleb," she began, her own voice a little softer. "I really don't want to do this now."

"Then come back to work tomorrow."

"I can't."

"You have to."

"No, I don't."

"You still have things left to do."

"I finished them."

"I don't think so. Sammi, I need you." Her eyes shot up to his face. He cleared his throat. "I need you to come back. There's still a lot to be done." She opened the door a little wider.

"There's nothing left to do that you can't do yourself, Caleb. You don't need me."

There was silence for a few seconds, and Sammi tore her gaze away from his face. Finally.

"Look." He shoved a piece of paper up against the screen door.

"What's that?"

"Open the damn screen door and take it, Sammi."

His agitation forced her to look back at him.

"Please?"

Resigned, Sammi flipped the latch on the screen door and cracked it open. He stuck the paper through, and Sammi took it.

It was her To Do List. Oh, God, she thought, he's been playing with the computer.

"Caleb, what have you done to the computer? You didn't mess up anything, did you?"

He smiled a little. Sammi tried to ignore it.

"Well?"

"I'm pretty sure I didn't mess up too much. I hope. Maybe you should come back and check it out. Maybe you could finish up those things on your list, too." His gaze caught hers for a moment. "If you feel comfortable doing that," he added quietly.

She thought about it for a few seconds. She didn't want to go back, and she *did* want to go back. Working with Caleb had made her happy, even if she wasn't exactly sure why. Though Sammi knew she was the person who liked to feel sure about everything. And safe.

What was the alternative? Sitting on her back porch, night after night, staring at beautiful sunsets—and having no one to share that beauty with. Sammi decided.

"Okay, I'll be there. Eight o'clock in the morning."

She eased the door closed, but Caleb's voice stopped her.

"Sammi—thanks. I'm glad you're coming back."

She watched his eyes, or what she could see of them through the dim light and screen door, anyway. There was always something in his eyes that she couldn't define, that kept her wondering. Something she'd never seen before in anyone else's eyes....

She nodded. "I'll see you in the morning."

Sammi was nervous. Here she was, back at square one, starting all over again with Caleb. At least that's how she felt. Of course, they knew each other a little better than on the first day she stepped into the clinic. And she knew her job responsibilities better. She knew exactly where to dig in this morning, what needed to be done. But she was still nervous.

How was he going to react? What would he say to her? How would she explain the weird relationship she had with her mother? And how would she ever explain how that relationship had hurt her over the years?

She didn't know. She just hoped he wouldn't bring it up, that he would let the subject of their accidental encounter drop and never mention it again. And she hoped that her mother would decide to go off on one of her cruises or something with one of her male *friends*, as she liked to call them. Then, at least Sammi would know she was safely out of the way—temporarily at least.

Oh, she loved her mother, in a way. And perhaps Desiree loved her, Sammi thought, but she had never been a proper mother. Desiree Jamieson had always been too wrapped up in herself to care much about anyone else. But then, Sammi had to wonder. Maybe it wasn't all her mother's fault. It must have been hard being married to a man she didn't love—but when he died and she could freely spend his money, her mother hadn't complained.

Her mother had never told her she didn't love Jack Jamieson. Sammi just deduced that fact on her own.

Things were said, overheard, and even long ago, Sammi could put two and two together. Jack Jamieson was twenty-five years Desiree's senior and had never been married. He wanted a wife and a child, and he was rich. He'd made profitable investments in real estate for several years. By the time he married Desiree, a poor but beautiful girl from the wrong side of the tracks, he had built himself a significant nest egg. Sammi was born the next year, and within months, Jack Jamieson had died of a heart attack. Sammi had absolutely no recollection of him.

But she didn't want to share all that with Caleb. There was no need. He didn't have to know the intimate secrets of her mundane life. She was sure he wouldn't be interested. So, she'd practically decided the night before that she should just continue to do her job at the clinic until she finished the last item on the To Do List, and then her life would return to normal. Caleb would not be a part of her life. She wouldn't let that happen.

Her game plan was simply to be efficient, be on time, do her work, and then go home. No touching, no kissing, no falling in love with Caleb Wyatt.

She would *not* allow herself to fall in love with Caleb Wyatt.

Because unlike her mother, she really didn't need a man to make her happy. She could be happy all on her own.

Sammi jumped at the sound of a door slamming. She turned to face Caleb entering the clinic from the barn.

He grinned. "Hi, Sammi."

She smiled back, just a little. "Hi, Caleb."

He shoved his hands into his pockets. Sammi thought he looked like a little boy, sort of shy and unsure of himself. "I'm glad you're back."

Sammi felt her grin broaden. "Me, too." Oh heck, she told herself, this was not going as she planned.

"Well," Caleb began before she let that thought go any further, "I have a question to ask you." He stepped forward and grabbed her hand. "Come with me."

"Wha—?"

Before she knew it, Caleb was leading her out of the clinic and toward his pickup truck. "What are we doing?"

"Something different." He opened the door for her. "Get in. Please?"

Sammi felt her eyes widen, but she did as he asked.

After Caleb had given the door a good shove, Sammi wondered if her decision was wise. Before she could make sense of the past few seconds, Caleb had joined her in the truck cab, started the engine, and was pulling out of the driveway.

"Mind telling me where we're going?"

Caleb slowed the truck, checked for traffic, then eased onto the road. One corner of his mouth went up in that grin that was so typical of him—the one that made every bit of Sammi's willpower melt.

"I thought you might like to ride with me today. I've got a couple of patients to check on, and then I'd like to head into the city to order some pharmaceutical supplies. Then we could go for lunch. And then maybe after that—"

Sammi held up a hand. "Whoa!"

Caleb downshifted and glanced her way as they came to a curve. "What?"

"I said, whoa."

"Why?"

"I thought you wanted me to work today."

Caleb dropped his head in a nod. "Yes, I said that, didn't I?"

"Yes, you did. I can't work running all over the countryside. Take me back."

"Well, we're already on the way. You can work tomorrow."

"Caleb—"

"Besides," he hurriedly added. "You didn't let me finish. After lunch I thought we'd pick out paint for the waiting room and new furniture, and then I'd let you figure out what to do with the windows. That's work." He glanced at her again. "Isn't it? Those things were on your list, weren't they?"

Sammi had to admit that they were. "Yes, of course"

"So you'll be working then. Besides, I need help this morning."

"You do?"

"Yes, I do."

"Doing what?"

He glanced about nervously and raked his fingers through his hair. "Well, I need to check on Mrs. Pierson's poodle. Mrs. Pierson gets hysterical every time she thinks about poor Minnie getting nailed by Brute, John Thompson's husky. I could use you to keep Mrs. Pierson occupied while I check out the poodle. She's gonna have pups. Big pups. It upsets Mrs. Pierson just thinking about it. That's how I can use your help."

"You're kidding."

"No! No, I'm not kidding at all. Maybe you could just have a cup of tea with her or something."

If Sammi didn't know any better, she'd swear Caleb Wyatt was lying, that he was making up reasons for her to be with him.

"Okay, I'll have a cup of tea with the hysterical poodle owner. It's not in my job description, but you seem to make that up as you go along." She looked at Caleb again. "Are you hot?"

Caleb swiped a hand over his brow. "No. Not at all."

"You're perspiring."

He glanced her direction again. "I'm fine, Sammi."

"Maybe you have a fever. Are you ill?"

"Sammi, I'm fine."

"Then why are you acting so jumpy and nervous?"

"I'm not!"

Sammi just watched him. He drummed his fingers on the steering wheel and fidgeted in his seat. He glanced from side to side, caught her gaze, then glanced back at the road. His foot was tapping the accelerator.

"Caleb, you really don't need me to help with Mrs. Pierson, do you? I mean, she can have hysterics by herself without my help."

He slowed the truck and waited at a stop sign for another car to pass in front of them. He didn't look at her. "Of course, I need your help, Sammi. Why else would I bring you with me?"

"That's a good question."

He looked at her. "What's that supposed to mean?"

"I wish I knew."

Someone behind them honked loudly three times. Caleb glanced in the rearview mirror, shakily shifted into gear, and the truck lurched forward. "Well, I'm sure I don't know what you're talking about."

Sammi lifted her chin and narrowed her gaze. Caleb Wyatt was a sneaky one, she realized just then. He'd got her to come back to the clinic today, and now he'd got her away from the clinic. The thing was, she didn't know why or didn't want to know why. Or maybe she knew why and just didn't want to admit it!

So, she let it drop. Whatever happened this morning, happened. The day was already set into motion, and she was powerless to stop it. Whatever Caleb had planned, she was just going to deal with it. And she would.

Chapter Nine

They stopped at Mrs. Pierson's. Her poodle was doing fine. Mrs. P. required soothing with a cup of tea, but Sammi felt she handled it all well, and they were on their way in no time. They also stopped to see a couple of Caleb's other patients, and they, too, were all doing well, too. The Marshall's foal was frolicking in the paddock when they arrived. The Henrys' newborn calf seemed to be bright-eyed and bushy-tailed. And even though Ryan Campbell's iguana still sported a yellow stripe, the reptile appeared to be as healthy as a horse. Or at least as healthy as a reptile.

Though, Sammi wondered if Caleb was just going through the motions. He could have done all these tasks without her. He hadn't really needed her help during this brief excursion. And it made her wonder—just what was Caleb Wyatt up to this morning?

Then they went for lunch, grabbing a quick bite from a food truck parked downtown by the Town Hall. Sammi recalled of her mother's invitation to Caleb to eat at the club, and his barely polite refusal. Twice, she smiled, thinking of how Caleb could easily put her mother in her place, if he so desired. Then thought him too much of a gentleman to stoop to her mother's level.

That was a good thing.

After lunch, they'd headed to the local discount store where they purchased paint and painting supplies. Caleb had set aside the next day for painting.

After that, they started for the farm.

It was a whirlwind day, and Sammi had to admit that she was sorry it was over so quickly. In fact, she really didn't want it to end at all.

But here they were, back at the clinic.

Sammi shut the door on the passenger's side of the truck, glanced once at Caleb, then turned toward her car. "I guess I'll see you in the morning, Caleb."

Caleb looked at his watch. "It's only three-thirty."

Sammi placed her hand on the door latch. She paused. "Yes, I guess it is."

She stood there, and Caleb didn't respond.

"You usually work until five," he finally said.

Sammi exhaled and turned back to look at him. "Oh. You're right. I just thought we were going to paint in the morning, and that there wouldn't really be anything to do until then."

Caleb shoved his hands into his pockets and glanced toward the clinic. "I have a question to ask you."

Caleb swallowed hard, and she waited. He crossed his arms. "I—" he began.

Sammi arched a brow. "Yes?"

"Sammi, I—"

She leaned forward a little in anticipation of his words.

"Sammi, would... Would you like to go out to dinner?"

She stepped back a bit. Dinner? Where the heck did that come from? Her mouth suddenly went dry, her hands went cold, and her heart stopped beating. Or maybe it just felt as if it had.

"Dinner?" she said again, inanely.

He nodded. "Yes. Tonight."

"To— Tonight?"

"Yes, ma'am, tonight. Would you like to go out to dinner with me? Tonight?"

Sammi felt the world begin a slow swirl around her. "Dinner?"

"Yes, Sammi. Dinner."

"But we already had lunch."

Caleb laughed. "I'm talking a nice dinner somewhere. Maybe a glass of wine and some music?"

Sammi blinked. There was nothing like that in Harbor Falls. "Yes," she heard a small voice say. She guessed it was hers. "Yes," she repeated.

Caleb grinned. That damnable crooked grin. Her heart jumped back into action again.

"Great. I'll pick you up at seven. Will that give you enough time?"

"Time?"

He laughed. "Yes. Time to get ready?"

She nodded. "Yes, that will be plenty of time." Of course, provided she could move from the very spot on which she stood. She seemed fused to the earth at that moment, incapable of movement.

"Well, I'll see you then."

Sammi smiled and nodded again. "Yes." Then quickly, she turned and headed for her car. Maybe she ran, she wasn't sure, she could have been skipping like a schoolgirl. Right before she slipped inside, she turned to face Caleb and gave him a smile and a brief wave.

Then she got in and drove toward home.

Oh boy. I have a date. A real date—with Dr. Caleb Wyatt.

—————

Sammi held a long floral skirt up in front of her, looked at herself in the mirror, and then tossed the thing onto the growing heap of clothing on her bed. *What am I doing? I don't date, and I have good reason for that. Why did I even say yes?*

And I don't have the right clothes.

Her stomach tied up in knots, jumping around like an out-of-control frog, legs flailing, she bit her lip and stared at the pile of fabric. The knots grew tighter, and the tension in her body only increased with every hop of that little frog.

Get a grip, Sammi.

Tossing a brown dress onto the pile, she fell backward into a sloppy heap on the bed next to the mountain of clothing. "I am an idiot. I should have said no."

She didn't date.

She liked her quiet, no-nonsense, uninterrupted, predictable, and otherwise routine life. She was prepared for things that way. Knowing what was happening next made her feel safe. It kept her out of the limelight, where she was most comfortable.

And she had her reasons. Good ones. Ever since she was a little girl, she craved the dark corner of the room while her mother happily claimed the spotlight.

Oh, crap. This was a mistake. Going out on a date with anyone, yet alone the new, handsome, veterinarian in town, was akin to jumping into a fishbowl.

Everyone would be watching. Looking at her. Because they knew she didn't date, too.

Small town. Where everyone knows everything....

Sitting up, she grappled in her pocket for her phone. "I have to break the date. I can't go."

Scrolling for Caleb's number, she took a deep breath, pressed the call button with her forefinger, and waited.

Straight to voice mail. Should she leave a message?

The bing sounded for her to leave one—but she sat silently staring at the phone.

She couldn't. She really didn't want to cancel. Did she? When was she going to be brave, go out on a limb, stretch her wings?

If not now, then when?

She pressed the end button, turned off her phone, and tossed it onto the bed along with the clothing.

Power through, Sammi. Figure it out.

She studied her closet. Work clothes on a dinner date wouldn't cut it. Her work clothes were too schoolmarmish. Her casual clothes were too casualish. Her Sunday clothes were too Sunday schoolish. There was nothing else.

Of course, she had no clue where he was taking her. They could go into Asheville, she supposed, but that was over ninety minutes away. Or perhaps they'd run out to the lake and have dinner at Lake Lodge. She'd heard dining on the deck out there was very nice. Most of the downtown restaurants closed after lunch, except for a new Italian restaurant she'd heard was opening soon. Asheville, yes. Maybe that's where they would be going.

What she needed was a little black dress. Didn't most women have a little black dress? It was a sure thing, she'd heard said. Wear pearls and heels to dress it up, flats and a jacket to dress it down?

A little black dress would give her confidence. Would it not?

She needed one. Then, when she saw Caleb step out of his truck in her driveway, she could have all the accessories ready to dress up, or down—depending, of course, on how he was dressed.

If he wore jeans? She'd go with the flats and a sweater and some costume jewelry.

If he wore dressier pants and a sport coat? She'd toss on the pearls and heels and grab a shawl wrap.

Okay. You've got a plan, Sammi.

Now—where would she find a little black dress on such short notice?

There was no dress shop in town, and Asheville was an hour away. No time. Only one other solution, which she hated, but she had no choice at this point.

Sammi took one last glance at her closet, the pile of useless clothing on her bed, and risked it. Right now, she'd go through hell and back for this one dinner date with Caleb Wyatt.

After all, it would probably only be one date. She might as well make it good and memorable.

And of course, she would not fall in love with him or anything—it was just a date, just dinner.

She was going to have a good time. It wasn't every day that a girl like her had dinner with a handsome veterinarian, right?

———

"You want to borrow what? Sammi, don't be silly."

Sammi's stomach churned. No, it did more than that. It belly-flopped into her intestines. A three-sixty, half-gainer dive right into the pit of her existence.

She shouldn't have come. This was a big mistake. Huge mistake. *Gargantuan* mistake. What the hell was wrong with her?

"Never mind, Mother, just forget it."

Desiree's face twitched. She hated rejection of any sort. And today, Sammi wasn't in the mood to humor her. She watched her mother light a cigarette and blow a stream of smoke to the ceiling.

"Now why in the world would you need to borrow a black dress?"

Sammi headed for the door.

"Sammi?"

She didn't look back. "Never mind, Mother, I'll find something else." What, she didn't know, but she would.

"Is there a funeral I should know about?"

Sammi stepped dead in her tracks, then moved. "No, Mother, there isn't a funeral. I'm going out to dinner."

One of Desiree's eyebrows arched. "Dinner?" She laughed. "Why on earth would you need my black dress to go out to dinner with your little sad-sack girlfriends?"

Sammi felt the chill go right through her. She shouldn't go there, take that bait. Still, she tilted her chin a little higher and replied, "I'm going out to dinner with Caleb."

The other brow arched then. "My, my... keeping company with the man, aren't you? Tell me, Sammi—is he good in bed? He has a very sexy grin. Come on, dear, we're both women, tell me."

Sammi felt her face flame with every shade of hot at her mother's words. *How dare she!*

"I wouldn't know, Mother. I don't impulsively hop into bed with men."

"Are you implying...?"

Sammi reached for the doorknob. "I'm implying nothing. I'll just be going now."

"So, you haven't slept with him yet, is that it?"

Sammi hadn't slept with any man, and she'd just about bet her mother knew that. From somewhere deep inside, Sammi found the courage not to crumble under her mother's words. "If I had slept with him, Mother, I'm sure you would be the last to know. And I can guarantee that I wouldn't be discussing it with you. I'm going now. Have a nice evening."

Sammi left the house.

Damn.

What an idiot I am.

CALEB WHISTLED AS HE PULLED THE FLATBED PICKUP into Sammi's drive. He couldn't remember the last time he'd whistled. Maybe it was because it had been an awfully long time since he'd felt this happy.

Sammi had agreed to go to dinner with him. Why hadn't he thought of this sooner? They were having an honest-to-goodness, real-live dinner date.

And it wasn't just your ordinary, run-of-the-mill dinner date either. No, Sir. He had other things in mind. Nothing else would do. Tonight was going to be a special night.

Glancing one last time at his reflection in the mirror, Caleb gave the collar of his shirt a last-minute tug and combed a couple of fingers through his hair to put it back into place. He pulled down the visor in front of him to hook his sunglasses there, and the letter with the Montana postmark fell in his lap.

He froze and picked it up.

Dammit. He'd forgotten about that one. It came in yesterday's mail. Stifling the sudden anger that threatened to ruin his good mood, Caleb stuffed the letter deep into the glove box and vowed to get rid of it, and the others, as soon as possible.

Montana was history, and he was moving on.

After looking long at Sammi's front door, he got out of the truck and quietly shut the door. Stooping, he bent to whisk some imaginary dust off his boots, then took a deep breath.

Are you procrastinating old boy? Don't let Montana ruin your evening.

He nodded to himself, shaking off the feeling, and walked up Sammi's sidewalk.

IF SHE WOULD LET HERSELF, SAMMI THOUGHT SHE might cry. It was almost time for Caleb to arrive, and she wasn't ready—and she wouldn't be ready. She wasn't going. She had nothing to wear.

Then Sammi stood and walked to her closet once more. Quickly, she rifled through the hanging clothes until she had pushed away all but the last dress in the closet, one that she'd almost forgotten.

Sammi reached for the robin-egg-blue cotton dress and pulled it out of the closet. The sundress. The one she'd worn last summer to some party her mother had dragged her to at the club. She'd hated the party but had loved the dress.

Sadly, she'd only worn it that one time.

It would do.

Smiling, Sammi fingered the thin spaghetti straps. Yes, this could be perfect. The dress, a pair of sandals, a little jewelry, and she would look—well, probably pretty good.

For her.

Sammi slipped her robe off her shoulders and the dress over her head. Just as she slipped her foot into a sandal, a knock sounded at the door.

Thank goodness she'd already done her hair and makeup.

Taking a deep breath, and then blowing it out, she stared into the full-length mirror.

"Now or never, Sammi," she whispered. "Go for it."

Chapter Ten

"Hi."

Sammi opened the door, and Caleb stepped inside. For a long, breathless moment, he simply admired her. Sammi's cheeks went hot.

Was he nervous too?

"I like that dress," he finally said, then blushed. "You look lovely, Sammi."

She glanced down at herself, glad she didn't own a little black number after all. "Thank you," she replied in a soft voice. "You look nice, too." He was dressed casually, newer starched jeans, cowboy boots, and a crisp button-down collar shirt, light blue. It matched her dress.

They looked like a couple. Sammi sighed. Did she want to be part of a couple?

"Are you ready?"

She glanced up to catch Caleb's eyes again and nodded. His gaze was warm and comfortable, and a bit sexy. Sammi smiled hesitantly, and he offered his arm. He hesitated only a second, then took it. Caleb closed the door behind them, and they headed for the truck.

The drive into town was silent for a while, as though neither of them could think of anything to say. But that was fine with Sammi, and it felt comfortable. She smiled inwardly. They'd spent days together at the clinic, and now it seemed as if they were meeting for the first time. Of course, it was their *first official* date, and they were both nervous. That was obvious.

Caleb continued to drive. Sammi said nothing until she realized they were heading back to his farm.

"Caleb—" she started.

"Sammi," he interrupted, "I hope you don't mind, but we're going to have dinner here." He glanced sideways at her. "Is that okay?"

That was more than okay. Sammi smiled. In fact, she preferred it that way. Suddenly, she wanted Caleb all to herself. She didn't want to share him. She especially didn't want to be on display in the fishbowl with him tonight. Had he sensed her hesitancy?

"That's fine. Perfect, actually."

He grinned back. "Good."

He pulled up next to the back door, rounded the truck cab, and offered her a hand after opening her door. As they stepped up the back steps to the house, Sammi realized it was the first time she'd ever been inside the farmhouse.

They entered the kitchen. A wonderful aroma swept over her. As she stepped into the room, a homey warmth and a sudden feeling of comfort enveloped her.

She liked Caleb's kitchen. Turning, she looked over at him. "Did you cook?" She remembered the day at the grocery store.

He walked into the kitchen. "Yes, ma'am, I did. I hope you like Italian." He reached into a cabinet over the sink and brought down two wine glasses.

"Yes, I love Italian."

"Good. Because it's my favorite." Reaching for a corkscrew on the counter, he removed the cork from a bottle of red wine, then slowly poured each of them a glass. He handed Sammi hers. "I hope you like red."

Sammi hated to admit that she knew little about wine, so she took the glass from him and smiled. "I'm sure it's fine."

Caleb glanced at the kitchen clock, peeked quickly in the oven, and looked back at her. "We've got a few minutes. Would you like to sit down?"

She nodded and said, "Yes."

Caleb placed a hand at the small of her back and led her into the next room.

Sammi was amazed at the condition of the farmhouse. From the outside, it looked as though it needed work, but the inside was quite cozy and looked recently renovated. She sat on the couch. Caleb sat beside her.

"Did you call earlier? I noticed I missed a call from you."

Her stomach clutched. She waved her hand, trying to act nonchalant, but inwardly hoping to ward away the baby frogs that were jumping around in there again. "Oh, it was nothing important."

"You're sure?"

She nodded. "Um-hm. Everything is fine."

He smiled, and Sammi sipped her wine. The more she drank, the more liked the flavor. "This is good. I like it. I'm not much of a wine connoisseur."

"No worries. I know only enough to make me dangerous. That's a Cabernet in case you ever want to remember for the future."

She took another sip. "Good to know."

A few silent moments followed, then Sammi angled toward him. "When did you move here, Caleb?"

He turned her way too, perching his leg up on the couch a bit. "Late February. I bought the farm right after Christmas, but there were a few things I needed to tie up in Montana before I moved here."

"Montana? So that's where you moved from?" Sammi realized at that moment how little she really knew about Caleb.

He took a sip of his wine and glanced off. "Yes."

Sammi watched his face. She wanted to ask more, but should she? He sat silently for a few minutes, then turned back to look at her.

She decided to risk it. "Do you have family back there?"

Caleb dropped his chin in a nod. "Yes. I have an aunt and uncle who still live there. My parents died when I was a teenager. Auto accident. I lived with my aunt and uncle off and on since then, when I wasn't in school. After college, I stayed until I started working at a veterinary clinic there."

His words trailed off. Sammi watched his gaze lower to his wineglass. He swirled the burgundy liquid around several times, and she, too, watched, held spellbound by the motion.

"What brought you to Harbor Falls?"

Caleb lifted his head and looked straight into her eyes. For several heartbeats he stared at her, and for the first time, Sammi wasn't uneasy. She let him search her face. She wondered if he was contemplating something.

"There was a situation there," he began, "that I needed to get out of."

The bluntness of his words startled her. To say those few words gave her heart a tiny jolt was an understatement. She wasn't sure how she knew, but there was more to this story than he wanted to say right now. So, she didn't push it.

"I also wanted to set up my practice. To strike out on my own."

Sammi nodded and sipped her wine. She sensed Caleb had told her enough—for now. He wasn't prepared to go on about *the situation.* In time, she supposed she'd find out what that was.

He continued, though. "I did some research, learned this area needed good veterinary services, and started looking for a place to set up practice. Harbor Falls was my second choice."

"Oh?"

He nodded.

"And you're first choice?"

"A little place in West Virginia, tucked into the mountains. Beautiful spot, but I lost the bid in a bidding war, so Harbor Falls it was."

Sammi smiled. "Lucky for us."

He grinned back. "Lucky for me." He grasped her hand.

Sammi felt the heat rise in her cheeks.

Changing the subject, Caleb asked, "Do you like it? The wine?" He dropped her hand and lifted his glass to his lips and sipped.

She nodded.

"I'm not that into wine," he admitted, "but I hoped this one would be okay. This seems like a good night to splurge."

Sammi grinned. "I don't drink wine very often either. Thank you. This is nice."

He smiled back.

Slowly, the awkwardness faded. Sammi glanced about. The warmth of the kitchen had spilled over into Caleb's family room—oversized furnishings, country decor, a welcome feeling. This is nice, she thought, comfortable.

"Did you renovate the house or was this already done when you bought it?"

Caleb glanced about. "I did it all. It was difficult working outside at the clinic in the winter months, so I didn't start there until the weather broke." He paused. "Would you like to see the rest of the house?"

Sammi's gaze played over his face. "Yes, I would love that."

She'd always been interested in older houses and their renovations.

They rose. About the same time, the timer on the oven went off. Caleb shrugged. "Maybe we should postpone the tour until after dinner. Let me check that."

Sammi agreed and followed him back into the kitchen.

DINNER WAS A WONDERFULLY GOOEY LASAGNA, A crisp salad, crusty bread, and the wine. They shared pleasant conversations, talking a bit about themselves, discussing some aspects of their lives. Nothing too intimate, too personal, but important things to know. After dinner, Sammi felt completely relaxed. Caleb offered her sherbet for dessert, but she declined. "I've more than exceeded my calorie limit."

Caleb grinned. "As have I. But I'm sure I'll be running on a deficit come Monday."

"You keep busy."

"I've kept you busy too, lately."

Sammi's gaze skittered off his. "I haven't minded."

They sat for a few minutes, sipping their wine in silence. When Sammi looked up, she noticed Caleb staring at her. Seemed he was always focusing his attention on her, which was both pleasant and difficult to get used to at the same time.

"May I ask you a question?"

Sammi studied him, then slowly shook her head. "Of course. I don't mind."

Caleb glanced at the tabletop for a minute or two, then let his gaze drift back up to meet hers. "Will you tell me about your mother?"

Sammi felt her backbone stiffen.

"What I mean," he went on quickly, "is that I want you to tell me about what happened the other day in the clinic. Your mother came in, and you nearly collapsed after she left. You were so upset, and I, well… It's none of my business, really, but I'm just concerned and wondered if you would tell me why."

Sammi didn't know if there would ever be a more trouble-some question she would have to answer. What could she say? That her mother had always seen Sammi as a disappointment? How could she explain?

She drifted off, staring at the seams of the wooden planks on the floor. And wished, at that moment, that she could slide through the cracks.

"Sammi?" he questioned.

Taking a deep breath, Sammi looked at Caleb. "My mother isn't a topic I usually discuss at dinner, but since you've asked, I'll answer. Briefly. Desiree Jamieson has always looked out for one person—herself. And all my life, I was second best. I was never good enough, never pretty enough, and never smart enough. Desiree had to be the best of every-thing. No way I could compete. And to this day, it's still the same, even now that I'm an adult. She's critical and manipula-tive. She has to get her way. And if I can help it, I stay away from her as much as possible." She paused, glancing away. "And that, Dr. Wyatt, is the short story of my relationship with my mother. I hope you can see why I really don't like to discuss it."

Sammi held Caleb's gaze. He stared deep into her eyes, perhaps somehow understanding. She hoped so.

He reached for and touched her forearm. "Your mother has really done a number on you over the years, hasn't she?"

Sammi snorted and glanced away. "I'm fine, Caleb. I'm a grown woman now. She can't hurt me anymore."

"She can't?"

"No, she can't."

And for a moment or two, Sammi almost believed it.

The room echoed with the silence that enveloped each of

them at that point. Finally, Caleb rose. "All right. I can tell that subject is not something you want to talk about right now."

Sammi nodded and stood as well. Searching his eyes, she added, "It's not something I want to discuss tonight. Or maybe ever, Caleb, to be perfectly honest."

He studied her for a moment. "There is one more thing I want to say."

Waiting for him to continue, Sammi held his gaze. It was a hard thing to do, but for some reason, she thought it was important.

Caleb took a couple of steps closer. Just close enough that Sammi's breath caught as his gaze deepened. Lifting a hand, he softly trailed the backs of his knuckles over her cheek and whispered. "I think you're beautiful. I also think you're intelligent, kind, soft-hearted, and nowhere near second best."

Sammi swallowed, then bit her bottom lip slightly. It was the closest thing she could get to pinching herself. Caleb thought she was pretty? Tears stung her eyes.

He moved closer. "I mean every word of that, Sammi."

"Thank you, Caleb," she murmured.

"You're welcome." Caleb wrapped his arms around her and pulled her into his embrace. She inhaled a sexy combination of body wash and a hint of cologne. She breathed in once more and held her breath. Nice. This was nice.

His holding her made her feel safe, secure. Cared for. *He thinks I'm pretty?*

Caleb stepped back and released her. Picking up both glasses of wine, he grinned and then handed one to her. Taking her hand, he led her into a smaller room, perhaps a family room or den, she thought, where the mood abruptly shifted.

She was relieved—she had no intention of continuing a conversation about her mother. But the other part, when he said all those wonderful things about her, that he thought she was pretty, and smart... She could listen to that stuff all night long.

And when he looked into her eyes, she could feel it to her toes.

"You big lug."

"What? Oh." She was lost in her daydream. Sammi glanced down. Caleb poked a finger at Goober, who had claimed residence on the couch. The dog lifted heavy eyelids. Turning to her, Caleb shrugged. "I don't think dynamite would move him."

Grinning, Sammi replied, "Well, perhaps it's time for the house tour then."

He nodded and reached for Sammi's wineglass and set both on the table beside the couch. "Good idea. This way." He swept his arms to one side and grinned.

Sammi stepped ahead, and Caleb followed.

"I guess we're doing this backwards," he said. "Starting at the back of the house and moving toward the front. We just left my small TV room, or den. The next one is the living room."

Sammi stepped into the large, sparsely furnished room. There were a lot of wood, walls, and beams. She could see the trees in the front yard through the old, oversized windows—one of the historic architectural features she loved of many older farmhouses in the area.

"I haven't had the time to decorate and realize the space wants for a little something."

A woman's touch. Sammi smiled and stepped toward a massive fireplace. "You've been busy, Caleb. I'm surprised you've accomplished as much as you have." She ran a finger along the oak mantelpiece. "I love oak. This is nice."

"It's the original mantel," he replied. "It was painted a hideous white that had yellowed over the years. I stripped the paint and found a beautiful golden oak underneath."

Sammi turned her gaze his way. Caleb drank in the softness of her eyes. "It's beautiful. Was it difficult to strip?"

"Not very. So you like oak?"

She nodded. "Oh, yes. I have several antique pieces of oak furniture."

"Is that a fact? Well, then, let's see what you think of this."

CALEB GRASPED SAMMI'S HAND. SOFT AND FEMININE, it was nearly lost encased within his big fingers. But he held it tight, not wanting to let her go as he led her to the staircase, and it didn't surprise him at all that she held onto his hand, just as tight.

"There is something I want to show you up here."

Her hand stayed firm within his as she followed behind. They topped the landing and stepped into the room on the left.

"Tell me what you think."

He watched Sammi, her gaze playing over the furnishings in his bedroom. Immediately, she stepped to the massive oak chest of drawers and ran her hand along the top. Then she turned and took in all the furnishings. "My goodness, Caleb, these are beautiful."

He was glad she liked them. Why, he wasn't quite certain, but he was. "I'm proud of them," he said. "I bought and restored every piece. It's something I do on the side when I've got time on my hands."

Sammi studied his face, then turned toward the bed. "The headboard is gorgeous." She walked toward the tall, carved piece and touched the intricate carvings. "This must have taken you forever."

Caleb stepped next to her. "It's a beauty, isn't it? I found it at an antique store in the Artisan Mall downtown."

Sammi grinned and ran her fingers lightly over the refinished wood. "I like to browse that place."

"We should go sometime," he said. "I'm always up for browsing."

Her face lit up.

Had he actually hinted that they'd see more of each other beyond the clinic? He turned back to the headboard. "I stripped layers of heavy black lacquer off this piece. It was difficult to remove, but easier than paint. I love it." He ran a hand over the smooth wood, grazing her fingers.

"You should. It's beautiful."

Caleb let his gaze drop to Sammi's face. He held the connection there for a minute, then reached out and turned her fully toward him. He pushed a stray hair away from her forehead and let his hands settle at her elbows. "I'm glad you like it."

Her lips parted. "I do. Everything here is beautiful. I'm jealous. I wish I had some pieces like this myself."

Caleb said nothing for a moment. Oh, there were words he wanted to say, but he didn't dare. He wanted to say yes, the antiques were beautiful, but the room wouldn't be complete until he'd added one more element to it—her. Permanently.

Whoa, boy. Not yet.

Instead, he said, "I think you're beautiful, Sammi."

Instantly, she flushed. And he thought it made her even more beautiful. "I mean that, Sammi, you are."

She shook her head. "Caleb... I'm not—"

He silenced her with a finger on her lips. "Shh, now, I don't want to hear any protests. To me, you're the most beautiful woman in the world."

The emotion that flashed across her face startled him. He could tell she'd not been told that often, if at all, and he hated that. To him, she *was* the most beautiful woman alive.

Hesitantly, he pulled her closer, gripping her elbows

slightly. She moved into him, their bodies touching. And when Caleb could stand it no longer, he cupped her cheek in his hand and drew her face to his.

Their mouths touched, briefly at first, then again. Sammi's tongue slid along his lower lip, and all Caleb could do was wrap his arms around her tighter and deepen the kiss. Hungrily, he took her again and, just as hungrily, she returned his kiss. Within seconds, Sammi's arms wrapped around his neck as she leaned into him.

Their mouths fused, their tongues parried, as they kissed.

Caleb broke away for a second and gasped. "Sammi..." He peered deep into her eyes.

"What, Caleb?"

"Come here."

He put one knee up on his bed and drew Sammi into his side. Slowly, he pulled her down next to him on the bed and settled her slightly beneath him. "I like kissing you," he said as he searched her face.

"Then kiss me some more?"

"That sounds like a question. Are you sure?"

Slowly, Sammi nodded. "Yes. Please kiss me, Caleb."

And he did.

To say she felt so right beneath him was an understatement. She felt more than right. It was where she belonged, and Caleb knew it. He only hoped she knew it, too.

Breathing deeply, he drew back, looking into her sweet face. He traced her lower lip with his finger then drew that finger along her cheek and down her neck. She trembled beneath him as he laid his palm flat on her chest and slipped his fingers underneath the thin straps of her sundress.

Her skin was so soft, and its silky feel nearly melted him. "God, Sammi, you are so damn beautiful," he whispered.

SHE COULD ONLY DRINK IN THE ESSENCE OF CALEB. All she could do was lay there next to him, looking up into his face, and absorb all the feelings that coursed through her body.

Her skin tingled where he touched her. Her lips, swollen from his kisses, wanted more of him. And her heart—her heart was beating way out of control, and her breathing was much too shallow.

All she knew at that moment was that she wanted it. All of it, and more.

His hand slid lower beneath the skinny straps and slightly over her breast. Then he descended on her again, and she rose to meet him. Hungrily, she devoured him, her arms reaching up to pull him closer to her, his hand gently squeezing and caressing her breast.

Then he broke the kiss and exhaled. His lips didn't leave her though. He simply kissed his way down her neck, to her collarbone, and then lower, to where his fingers were now teasing her nipple.

The strap of her dress had slipped off her shoulder, and Caleb caressed her breast with his mouth, gently at first, then finally taking her fully inside and sucking hungrily at her tender and now swollen nipple.

Sammi's breathing was coming fast and hard. Never had she felt like this, ever. The sensations that washed over her were foreign and unreal—yet so full of love and passion she knew they had to be real.

She wanted Caleb, and it scared her so much she nearly froze thinking about it.

She'd never made love to a man before.

Would Caleb know that? Would she be able to satisfy him? What if it were a terrible experience for him? For both? What if she didn't know what to do? What then? Would he ever want to see her again?

She wasn't sure if she could risk that.

"Caleb," she whispered.

"Oh God, Sammi, you feel so good."

He kissed her breast, then looked into her face. "I want to make love to you, Sammi," he told her. "I want to make love to you in my bed. Here. Now."

Sammi gulped in a breath and searched his face. She wanted him to make love to her, wanted it more than anything, but she couldn't, not now.

Maybe never.

Reaching out, she touched his face and gently caressed his cheek.

She huffed out a quick breath. "Caleb...."

His eyes darted back and forth, and he waited.

"I...I've never. I...can't."

She wasn't sure how she got the words out, but she finally did.

He simply looked at her for another moment, then dropped his head. Next, he lifted her sundress strap back up onto her shoulder and moved off her, offering her a hand as they got back up off the bed.

"Then I'd be honored to be your first lover, Sammi," he murmured. "But only if you are sure that's what you want. I'm following your lead, sweetheart."

Her gaze held his for several rapid beats of her heart. "No. Not tonight. I'm sorry, Caleb."

He nodded. Sammi wasn't sure what the nod meant.

Then he took her home.

Chapter Eleven

C aleb couldn't sleep. He didn't know why he wasn't used to it by now, since he hadn't slept a full night since Sammi had come into his life. Especially lately. So, he got up, dressed, and headed for the clinic.

Within the hour, he had moved all the chairs away from the wall, covered the floor with plastic, removed all the electrical outlet and switch plate covers, and was ready to paint. He figured physical work was the only thing that would get his mind off how he'd ruined everything with Sammi.

He wasn't sure what had gone wrong last night, but the only thing he could think of was that it was his fault. It had to be. He was moving too fast for her, obviously.

He decided not to dwell on it, but he couldn't lie there in that big old bed any longer, remembering how Sammi had admired it and how she'd felt beneath him. How he'd wanted her to be there permanently. And because of his urgency, he'd made a mistake. He'd told her he wanted to make love to her. That was the truth, and he wouldn't deny it. He wanted to make love to her. He loved her, dammit! Shouldn't he want to make love to the woman he loved?

But you shouldn't have told her that, stupid.

Caleb smacked himself on the forehead. "Oh hell, you are an idiot."

He hadn't told her he loved her. A woman like Sammi deserved that, didn't she? Especially when it was true.

He would have to remedy the situation. The first chance he got.

SAMMI DECIDED EARLY THAT MORNING THAT IT WAS time to change her life. She was tired of being mousy. Tired of being shy. Tired of always worrying about what other people thought.

But most of all, she'd grown weary of waiting around for her life to get interesting. Dammit! Life had nearly gotten interesting last night, and she'd blown it!

It wouldn't happen again. Likely. Not in her lifetime.

Unless she made it happen.

She was up and dressed way before dawn. She didn't even have to think twice about what to wear. The plan for the day was to paint, if she recalled, so she donned her oldest, albeit tightest, blue jeans and tied an old, soft denim shirt up around her waist. But underneath...ah, well, that's where things got interesting.

Sammi always bought pretty lingerie, except she'd never really worn them all that much. It seemed somewhat useless. Today, though, she slipped into her sexiest red lacy bra and panties before dressing in her work clothes. If she were going to surprise Caleb, then she might as well go all the way. And that's what she planned to do—go all the way.

After she pulled her hair into a bouncy ponytail, Sammi applied just a hint of blush to her cheeks, a little mascara to her lashes, and a bit of gloss to her lips. Now, she was ready.

She didn't expect to see the lights on in the clinic as she pulled into Caleb's drive, but they were on now. It was unusual to see Caleb up and about. He usually sauntered into the clinic just before eight, and it was barely seven o'clock.

As she stood beside her car, Sammi took a deep breath, exhaled, looked long at the clinic, then decided that if this was going to be the last day of her virginity, she might as well get it over with as soon as possible.

Not that she was dreading it. It was high time. And she was glad, for once, that she'd waited for the right man to come along; that she had waited for Caleb.

Besides, she had to do it now before she lost her nerve.

She pushed open the clinic door. The room was a mess. Stuff was everywhere.

Caleb turned at the sound of the door closing.

"Morning, Caleb." She rushed into the room, stood beside him, hands on hips, and surveyed what he'd accomplished so far. Obviously, he couldn't sleep either.

"So, you're up early too, huh?"

Caleb looked at her and swallowed, his Adam's apple bobbing. His gaze raked up and down her form, and Sammi almost laughed aloud. It was the reaction she wanted. She knew the jeans were tight, and she knew the shirt tied at her middle accented her hips and waist nicely. And she knew that if she'd caught Caleb Wyatt's attention yesterday in the dowdy clothes she'd been wearing to work for the past few weeks, the skintight jeans would send him over the edge.

"Way early."

She picked up a paint roller. "You didn't wait for me."

"I had to do something." He looked her up and down once more. "I needed something to do with my hands."

Sammi flashed him her biggest smile, then she sidled up next to him. "If you're having trouble deciding what to do with those big hands, let me know. I might think of something."

It was probably the boldest thing she'd ever said to a man in her entire life. And if she hadn't been so secure in knowing how Caleb felt about her, she never could have said it. She'd thought long and hard throughout the night and realized that Caleb's actions of late showed he cared for her.

And she knew she mirrored those feelings for him.

For the first time in her life....

She sighed.

I'm in love.

She loved Caleb, and she wanted him to make love to her.

She dipped the roller in the paint pan, rolled it twice to load the paint, tapped it gently on the side of the pan, and looked back at Caleb. "Would you rather I work right here? Or should I move to the other side of the room?"

Caleb stared at her.

"I think I'd rather you put that thing down and come here."

HE WATCHED AS THE PAINT ROLLER IN HER HAND slowly lowered and the sassy look on her face suddenly turned to something else. Desire. Oh, God. She wanted him.

Finally!

The paint roller clanked to the floor. Droplets of paint splattered everywhere. And all Caleb could think about was getting her into his bed before she changed his mind.

He wanted her. Right now, on the tarp, rolling around in the paint. Wanted to make wicked and delicious love to her before she changed *her* mind.

But he didn't want sex that way with her for their first

time. He wanted to claim her, convince her with his lovemaking, that she was his. He wanted her in his bed.

"Come here," he said, then grasped her hand and led her out of the clinic.

Without a word, they entered the house, ascended the stairs, and went straight to Caleb's bed. He turned her to him and searched her doe-like eyes. Everything about her appeared soft and full of passion. And he knew she wanted this as much as he did.

"I have to tell you something, Caleb," she whispered.

"No," he returned just as quietly, "I have to tell you something."

She shook her head, but Caleb bent forward and kissed her. The soft, brief touches of their lips sent chills down to his toes. God, how he wanted her, how he loved her. Pulling back, Caleb caressed her face with his fingertip as he looked deep into her eyes.

"I love you, Sammi," he said then. "I've loved you from the day you walked into my clinic."

He watched tears well up in her eyes. "Caleb—"

He kissed her again, afraid of what she was going to say. Had he misread her? This was what she wanted, wasn't it? Surely he'd correctly understood the signals she'd sent a few minutes ago.

The kiss deepened, and he found Sammi's arms wrapping more tightly around his neck and her body pressing oh-so-sensuously against his.

No, he wasn't mistaken. She wanted him as much as he wanted her.

She broke the kiss with a gasp. "Caleb," she whispered against his cheek. "I've never done this before."

As his hands stroked her back, Caleb took in her words, and he drew her closer to him. She'd never made love with a man before. He would be her first.

"I love you, Sammi. I won't hurt you."

When she drew back and looked into his eyes, Caleb knew she was giving him the most precious gift a woman could give a man. He cradled her head in his hands and kissed all over her face.

"I love you, too, Caleb. I trust you. I couldn't do this if those things weren't true."

And he knew in his heart that what she'd said was the truth. As difficult as it had been to convince Sammi of his love, she wouldn't give that love unless it was what she wanted.

"I will never hurt you, Sammi. Never."

She ran a palm over his cheek. "I know that." Then she leaned up and kissed him again. "Now, make love to me."

At last, she was his. Caleb reached for the buttons of her denim shirt and slowly opened first one and then the other, making his descent to the knotted tails at her waist. He watched as glimpses of red satin and lace peeked out at him from beneath the denim, and he looked once more into her face. She wanted him. She'd planned this. And as his breathing grew heavier with each button released, he knew this moment would stay with him forever.

He made quick work of the knot, then slipped the shirt off her shoulders and into a heap on the floor. Sammi's eyes closed as he descended upon her throat, kissing his way down to the red lace covering her breasts. He put his hands on her waist and drew her close, inhaling her feminine scent. He knew that by the end of the day, Sammi would be his for all time.

She bunched his shirt into her fists at his waist, pulling him closer. Caleb groaned. "You're driving me crazy," he breathed against her chest.

His fingers went to her waist and popped the button on her jeans, then slowly inched the zipper downward. He slid his hands inside her jeans and exhaled as his palms touched her velvet skin.

Sammi reached up, cupped her hands around his face, and angled her mouth across his. "I want you," she whispered against his lips.

Caleb needed no further prodding. For a woman with no experience, she seemed to know instinctively just what to do to make a man crazy with desire.

He wasted no time sliding the tight jeans down over her hips, his hands slipping inside her red satin panties, removing both garments at the same time. Caressingly, he slid denim and lace down over her silky legs, then crouched to remove her canvas tennis shoes, and then each leg of her jeans. He rose slowly, kissing first her knees, then inching upward to her thigh, then breathing deeply as his lips graced her sex.

He could feel Sammi trembling. He rose then and looked longingly into her eyes while his fingers played gently between her legs. She gasped, breathing quickly, looking up at him. Finally, he urged her closer to the bed and gently laid her there. Before he joined her, he quickly shed his own clothing.

Sammi watched Caleb undress. His fingers moved deftly over his buttons as he made short work of removing all his clothing. She was glad he hurried. She wanted him next to her, on top of her, inside of her.

Caleb's body warmed hers as he joined her on the bed. His chest felt so right next to hers. His lips, now playing beneath her ear, were warm and silky and made her want him more. He angled up on one elbow and peered down in her face. She watched his eyes as she felt his fingers lightly graze over her breasts. Slowly, he lazily trailed the finger down to her belly, circling her navel, and again, she watched his gaze follow the path he was making on her body.

His fingers grazed lower until they reached the apex of her thighs and once there, he gently parted her legs and slowly massaged and rubbed her there. Sammi gasped at the sensations reeling through her body. She turned into his chest and closed her eyes, breathing deeply of his male essence. He lowered his lips to her ear and whispered softly.

"We're taking this slowly, Sammi. I want you to be ready for me. I want you to feel everything. Close your eyes, hold on to me, and just let me take care of you."

Caleb increased the pressure between her legs then, and she quickly nodded and involuntarily arched toward him. "Yes," she whispered.

She felt a finger slowly slip inside of her, gently caressing, making small circles, and as she closed her eyes and simply let the sensations roll over her, Sammi felt herself falling more and more in love with Caleb. For the first time in her life, she was forgetting everything else and simply being herself. And allowing herself to feel what she genuinely wanted to feel.

She opened her eyes and looked up into Caleb's face. He was watching her. He probed more deeply into her, and she shuddered. Caleb's face was full of something she couldn't describe. And even though she almost felt as though she should be embarrassed by what she was feeling, by what he was doing to her, the look on his face told her that what they were doing was natural and beautiful.

He leaned forward then and lightly kissed her lips. As his fingers gently played and probed and massaged, the kiss deepened. Caleb thrust his tongue into Sammi's mouth, and she eagerly took it, wanting him. All of him.

She broke the kiss. "I want you, Caleb," she gasped.

She didn't have to ask again.

Caleb rolled over on top of her, nudged her knees apart, and settled himself between her legs. They kissed again, their mouths and tongues merging and joining, as his hands and hers moved and touched along the contours of each other's bodies. He probed then, gently, between her thighs until

Sammi felt him at the center of her sex, and she knew he was holding back. Taking both hands to his face, she lifted his head so she could look into his eyes. She kissed him then, and said, "Take me, Caleb. I'm yours."

Caleb groaned.

There was a gentle, and then more urgent, push into her body. Sammi stilled at the initial plunge and clutched at him until the slight pain subsided. Then she slowly joined in his motion, swelled to his touch, opened to let him in, fully, as he moved rhythmically inside her.

Sammi found her breathing coming in irregular spurts, small gasps that were shallow and slight. Then the pressure built as Caleb pushed into her over and over; she clung to him, arching into his body, meeting his every thrust, easing out small squeaks of pleasure. She barely registered the fact that Caleb had lifted slightly off her and was watching her face.

The crescendo inside her built to a flurry of pleasure. Her body involuntarily took the lead, and her self-consciousness left her. An orgasm welled up, spilled over, and chased throughout her body. She clutched at Caleb's biceps and shouted out his name.

At some point she heard him shout her name, too, felt him plunge deep into her core, and pull her body into his. He pinned her there against the bed as they pulsated, both crying out, trembling, exhausted. She was spent, sated, and happy, attempting to come down from somewhere she had never been before.

She hoped he felt the same.

Chapter Twelve

Sammi stretched lazily, then nestled against Caleb's side. Slowly, recognition of all that had happened in the past twenty-four hours settled over her.

She was Caleb's woman now. He'd made her his repeatedly. And he'd told her so every time he took her. Throughout the day and deep into the night, they'd made passionate love. Every touch, every kiss, every heated stroke of their bodies only made her long for more. He'd thoroughly made love to her, and she had loved him back, body and soul.

Groggily, she lifted her head. Caleb lay beside her, still sleeping, his almost black hair tousled, and his mouth soft and relaxed.

He is beautiful. She laid her hand on his chest, perched her chin upon it, and watched him sleep. She knew she probably shouldn't think of him as beautiful, since most men had a macho attitude about the word. Women were beautiful, roses and sunsets were beautiful. Men? They were supposed to be something else. Strong. Handsome. Striking.

Sex.

He was all that, too.

But to her, Caleb was beautiful. When he'd undressed for her the morning before and had lain beside her, she'd ached to touch his body. So timid, she only let him pleasure her, and then as the day progressed into the night, she'd allowed herself to become bolder, daring to touch him, to please him. Kiss him in places she'd previously thought unimaginable.

And she liked it.

It was easy for her to do that. He made it so easy for her. For once in her life, Sammi was glad she'd waited—for Caleb. Glad her first lovemaking had been with a man who was so giving and so willing to teach.

And teach he did, throughout the day, and the night.

Reaching up, she traced along his upper lip with her forefinger, then let it slide slowly down his chin. Caleb brushed away what she supposed felt like a tickling sensation with his hand, without opening an eye. Sammi smiled. She could lie there and watch him all day.

But she didn't. She lazily let her hand move over his chest, the pads of her fingers softly caressing the smooth muscles there, then circling an erect nipple on either side. She watched his muscles contract and relax as she touched him. Then she flattened her palm and smoothed her hand over his belly, flat, firm, and warm. She caressed him gently and moved lower.

When she reached his thighs, she stopped and looked back up into his face. His eyes were still closed. She watched him for a minute, then softly ran a finger up his hard length.

He was beautiful. He was the most beautiful man she'd ever seen, and she loved him so.

Sammi kissed his chest, and he awoke. She lifted her gaze and smiled. "Wake up. I want more."

Groaning, Caleb grabbed her by both upper arms and flipped her over, pinning her against the bed. "You're insatiable," he growled, smiling.

Sammi grinned. "You made me that way."

He nuzzled her neck and pushed himself deeper between her legs. "I think I've created a monster."

She raked her fingernails down his back. "Um, a monster indeed."

Wincing just a little as he pushed inside her again, Sammi dismissed the momentary soreness and allowed her body to accommodate him as she'd done hours before.

"Sammi, honey," Caleb whispered. "I will not want to stop doing this anytime soon."

She matched his rhythm and gazed into his face. "I don't want you to stop," she breathed.

"I want you forever," Caleb said. "I want to be your *forever man*."

LATER, SAMMI STEPPED OUT OF CALEB'S SHOWER, towel-dried her hair, and then wrapped the huge green towel around her, tucking in one end at her breasts to anchor it. The mirror was steamy, so she borrowed Caleb's blow dryer to get rid of the steam, then fully dried her hair as she watched her reflection.

She almost didn't recognize the woman staring back at her.

A slow smile broke over her face, and a delightful giddiness welled up inside her.

This woman, she told herself, is who I am supposed to be. It had taken her a long time to reach this place, but she was here now, and she was glad.

She flushed at the thought of how Caleb had made her feel, the things he'd done to her body. Leaning forward, Sammi stared at herself in the mirror. She pinched her cheek.

It wasn't a dream.

"Ow," she said, then smiled at her reflection. "Yes, Sammi, this is real, you've finally fallen in love."

Grinning broadly, Sammi tilted her chin and tossed the mirror a sassy look. Yes, she was in love, and the best part of all was that Caleb loved her back.

And if she had to do it all over again, she wouldn't do it any other way.

She winked at herself and then tossed her hair back over her shoulders, tucked the towel more securely around her, and opened the door to find him.

IF THE SUN, MOON, STARS, AND EVERY SINGLE solitary planet in the universe had been handed to Caleb on a silver platter, he couldn't have been more ecstatic. In fact, he was more than that. He was delighted, thrilled, and yes, perhaps even overjoyed.

Making love to Sammi had surpassed all his fantasies. It had not mattered to him one iota that she was inexperienced. In fact, that alone had stimulated his passion—she was such a willing student, and he was a more than ardent teacher. And oh, how he relished teaching her more and more over the coming years.

He was sure he had found what he wanted. He wanted Sammi to be his wife, for all time and as soon as possible.

He knew, though, he should step lightly around the subject of marriage.

However....

Caleb glanced up as the bedroom door creaked open and Sammi stepped into the room. He felt the corner of his mouth twitch and parts of his anatomy that should be exhausted rose to attention. He wanted her again. Oh, God. Would it always be like this?

He didn't doubt that it would.

Sammi approached the bed with a sexy little grin on her face and stopped, letting the towel drop to the floor. She then slid back underneath the covers with him.

Caleb groaned. "You're gonna be the death of me, woman."

He winced as Sammi bit his lower lip. "No, you're young and healthy, Caleb. I don't think what I have in mind for you is fatal."

Caleb grasped her arms and pulled her on top of him. Sammi's legs immediately straddled his waist, then she scooted lower. Caleb could only sigh at the pleasure he knew he was about to receive.

Oh, God. My life will never be the same again.

"I think I should probably go home."

Sammi shifted to her side and perched her head up on a bent elbow. She gazed into Caleb's eyes as she added, "I bet Dicey is fit to be tied."

Caleb reached up and nuzzled her neck. Her eyes fluttered closed at the sensation. "The cat will be fine."

"She's had no food today, Caleb. Or fresh water."

He plopped back flat on the bed and stared at the ceiling. Slowly, he angled his gaze back to her. "You're right. I guess we do have to get up sometime."

Sammi slid back down next to him. "I don't want to leave here, Caleb, but you know we have to think about the babies."

Caleb arched a brow. "Babies?"

"I wonder when the due date is?"

"Sammi, I—"

She laughed then and said, "I'd think it would be soon. How many weeks has it been since that yellow tomcat got my poor girl?"

She watched as recognition settled over Caleb's face.

"I thought you meant—"

"Yeah, I know. I'm a tease."

His eyes twinkled. "That you are, my dear. So, you think Dicey's pregnant?"

She nodded. "I think so, but you're the best judge of that. She looks very round. I've been meaning to mention it to you."

Sitting up, Caleb rubbed his face and eyes as if to bring himself back to reality. "Okay. Let's go check on the cat, feed her, and then—"

Sammi leaned forward and placed her lips on his. "Then we can take a break in my bed," she whispered.

Caleb groaned.

Sammi smiled and backed off the bed, taking the sheet with her. In only one night, she'd come to love the sound of those groans.

THE CAT MET THEM AT THE BACK DOOR.

Dicey wanted to act with indifference, but she meowed and circled them both, rubbing her head against their legs, and even patting Sammi's legs with her front paws as she walked to the cabinet to retrieve her food.

They let the cat eat, watching her as they leaned against the counter. Occasionally, Dicey would glance up to look at them, just to make sure they were still there.

Finally, she lifted her head and stalked off without a glance in their direction.

"Well, that little priss!" Sammi remarked.

Caleb chuckled. "I can't say for sure, but I'll bet kittens are on the way, Sammi."

"You think so?" Suddenly, the idea of motherhood appealed to Sammi. She rushed into the family room and found Dicey cleaning her face next to the patio door. Sammi scooped up Dicey, cradling the cat in her arms. Caleb joined her.

After a minute of gently feeling and examining Dicey's belly, he nodded. "A couple of weeks, maybe," he told her.

Sammi raised Dicey to her cheek and nuzzled the cat. "You're gonna be a mommy, pumpkin." Then she looked at Caleb. "So what do I do?"

He shrugged. "She'll take care of things on her own. You could fix her a box if you wanted, but chances are she'll pick the place where she wants to deliver."

"On her own?"

"Sammi, haven't you ever had a pet before?"

She shook her head. "No. Dicey is my first."

Grinning, Caleb placed his hands on her waist, pulled her closer, then placed a quick kiss on her nose. "Then you're in for a treat. Kittens are fun, and Dicey will be a good mother."

Sammi scratched under the cat's chin. "Of course she will be, and I'll be here to help."

Caleb tightened his grip on her. Sammi looked back into his eyes. "I think you'll be a great mother too, someday."

Funny, Sammi thought, how she was thinking along those same lines herself. "Maybe someday," she answered softly, then gave Caleb a grin. She wasn't ready to take it any further than that. Heck, she'd just found out how wonderful lovemaking could be. It wasn't quite the time to think about procreation...yet.

"So, now that Dicey is fed, what are we going to do for the rest of the afternoon? I have an idea if you're game."

Sammi shrugged. "I haven't really thought—"

A knock sounded at the back door, and Sammi glanced in that direction. "Wonder who that could be?"

Caleb cocked his head sideways. "Haven't a clue. Why don't you go find out?"

Smiling, Sammi stepped back toward the kitchen, then

took another step forward to place a kiss on his lips. "Be back in a second. Here, you take the mommy."

She dumped Dicey into his arms. As she reached the back door, she got a glimpse of her mother's car in the driveway. An immediate sting of panic shot through her, but she wasn't sure why. She opened the door anyway.

Desiree breezed into the kitchen, glancing this way and that. "Sammi! My goodness. Don't you ever return your calls?"

"I just got in, Mother. I haven't checked yet. Is everything all right?"

Desiree eyed her, then continued. "Everything is fine, dear. It's just that I called late last night and I didn't get an answer, and I called early this morning and didn't get an answer, and Carol Martin told me she hadn't seen your car all day yesterday or last night, and I was worried."

Sammi had a hard time believing that, but after a second of studying her mother's face, she realized she was indeed worried. "Mom, I'm fine. See? I'm here and everything's fine. Don't worry."

"But where were you?"

Sammi cleared her throat, knowing that Caleb was probably listening in the next room. She didn't want to get into this right now with Desiree. Everything was too new. She wanted to savor it for a while before she and Caleb became the talk of the town.

"I was visiting a friend."

Her mother stared at her. "Usually, you let me know when you're going to be out of town."

"I—I wasn't exactly out of town. And it was...sort of sudden."

Her mother's inquisitive look was almost comical, and for a split second she wanted to tell her mother exactly where she'd been and what she was doing, but she wasn't ready.

Desiree's eyes narrowed. "You were with Caleb, weren't you?"

Sammi didn't immediately answer. She didn't know why she didn't want her mother to know. She just knew that right now, she didn't. When she finally opened her mouth to speak, Desiree abruptly added, "Well, just be careful, Sammi. A man like Caleb is going to need a woman who can keep him. I know you like him, dear, but be realistic. He probably needs a woman a little more sophisticated than you. After all, he has degrees. He's a doctor. So, have fun, but just don't go getting too attached, dear. You realize he will not want you around forever. I don't want you to get hurt."

There. That was the reason she hadn't wanted to tell her mother.

The stab that pierced Sammi's heart was almost more than she could take. She placed her hand there, to comfort herself. How could her mother—

"Well, hello, Mrs. Jamieson."

Caleb entered the kitchen, and Sammi wanted to bolt into his arms—but something stopped her and anchored her directly to the spot, melding her to the floor so she couldn't move.

The only thing she registered was her mother slowly turning toward the sound of Caleb's voice.

"Well, well, Dr. Wyatt."

Caleb nodded, then walked to Sammi's side and put an arm around her, holding her tight against him. Sammi placed one arm around his waist and raised the other to rest on his chest. She needed his support because, in about two seconds flat, she was going to burst into tears.

"Have you told your mother the news?"

His tone was soft, and Sammi sensed him looking down at her. After a second, Sammi lifted her gaze to look up at him. "News?" she whispered.

He grinned then, and Sammi suddenly knew everything would be all right.

"Oh, the news," she added, then looked at her mother.

Desiree's face was stony, unmoving, as she watched the two of them.

Caleb's voice was firm when he finally spoke. "We were going to come by this evening and tell you, Mrs. Jamieson. We're glad you're here now so we can share the news with you. Sammi and I are getting married."

Sammi felt a little fuzzy and dizzy and clutched at Caleb's shirt. She was trying to take in his words and her mother's expression at the same time. She looked back to search Caleb's face.

He slowly turned his gaze to her, and in a soft, sexy, very loving voice said, "It was going to be a surprise. We're going to look for a ring this afternoon. We love each other very much, and I'm looking forward to spending the rest of my life with your daughter."

Every sensation known to a woman sprang forth in Sammi then, and it didn't matter if her mother was in the room or not. "I love you, Caleb," she whispered.

"I love you, too, honey," he returned.

Then he leaned over to nuzzle her neck, on the side away from Desiree, and whispered, "Marry me?"

Nodding, Sammi softly responded, "Yes."

Chapter Thirteen

There were days she couldn't stop staring at the engagement ring on her left hand. Sammi stopped typing for a second and glanced down at the flash of light reflecting off her finger. She was used to the weight of it now. Though it wasn't heavy, there was a definite weightiness that she'd quickly grown accustomed to. As if it were supposed to be there.

And she was quite certain it *was* supposed to be there.

Caleb loved her more than she'd ever dreamed someone would. He showered her with attention, kisses, did little things to please her throughout the day, and made her feel like the most beautiful woman on earth. And when she was in his arms, that was exactly how she felt.

Rising, Sammi stepped across the clinic and looked out at the farmhouse through the open door. It had grown unusually cool the past few days, and she'd turned off the air conditioner, opting for open doors and windows to freshen up the place. She studied the house and smiled.

Caleb had done a good deal of work on the inside, but the house wasn't yet finished. He'd started tackling the outside as soon as they'd bought the ring and made it official that they were getting married. The date they'd set was a few months off, near Christmas in fact, but Caleb wanted the house finished before then. He told her that if he didn't get onto it immediately, he would likely never get it done in time. He wanted a home for Sammi, and he wanted it to be perfect.

Sammi knew his thinking was on track. With the clinic finished, more clients were coming in, and business would only pick up. Well, except for her mother's business. She had opted to take Pookie to Asheville for his poopsie problems.

So be it. Sammi couldn't be more pleased.

Caleb had also taken advantage of the seasonal weather to replace the siding and fix the roof before business took off and he had to hire someone else to do it.

She watched as he climbed the ladder and prepared to peel the old shingles from a section of the roof. He'd worked so hard the past month. They both had, actually. She had finished painting inside the clinic so he could start on the house, and she liked the fact that worked as a team to accomplish something.

They made an exceptionally good team.

Sammi thought about all Caleb had done to make their home together, and it warmed her heart. They had decided to live there, which was logical, being next to the clinic. Sammi would rent out her little cottage in town after they married. She was getting eager, though, to add some womanly touches to the old farmhouse, and Caleb had encouraged her to do so.

She'd not done much yet, except to clean out a few cabinets and add a throw pillow or two, but the nesting urge was getting stronger every day.

Sammi glanced at the office. The computer work could wait until tomorrow. It was time to take stock, make lists, and figure out what she wanted to do to make Caleb's home her home. Their home together. It was time.

Grinning and eager to get started, she rushed back to the computer, closed her file, and switched the thing off, happier and content than she had ever been in her entire life.

WIPING THE SWEAT FROM HIS BROW, CALEB TOOK A deep breath and looked up from his work to see Sammi heading across the yard from the clinic.

He smiled.

All his life, this was what he'd wanted. His parents had died when he was a kid, and he'd lived for a while with his aunt and uncle. They were wonderful to him, but he'd wanted his own home. It was the driving factor that led him to pursue his veterinary degree, and what had kept him going when times got bad.

Eight months ago, he'd just about figured he would never reach his dream. After that fiasco, he knew that if he was ever going to achieve the one thing in his life that he craved—a home and family—he was going to have to leave Montana and create a new life for himself.

So he did.

Buying the farm was the first step. He had to have a home before he could have a family. The thing was, he never dreamed that the woman of his dreams would come into his life now. He figured it would take him some time, a couple of years or more, to find her.

But here she was now, looking up at him and smiling and waving as she headed for the back door of the house that was soon to be *their* home.

And the thought of that made him feel that his life was finally coming together.

Sammi couldn't believe how disorganized Caleb could be. In some ways, he was highly organized, particularly in his work, but in others, he was totally disgusting. She'd figured that out when she'd straightened up his kitchen cabinets the other day. But this closet, that was something else.

Well, it shouldn't have been a surprise to her, considering how the office looked the first day she came here. Smiling, she figured she'd just have to overlook that aspect of Caleb's life. She was the efficient one. She could organize his life. His closets, too.

It looked as though he used the closet off the entrance for storage. Anything that didn't have a place was tossed in there. Sammi hadn't really planned to clean it. The matter was sort of forced upon her.

She was trying to figure out if there was enough room in the entrance for the antique oak hall tree she owned when she realized the closet was there. She'd opened the door to see how far back it would go, and how much space there was left, when boxes, shoes, boots, books, coats, a baseball bat, and several hats came tumbling out at her. The jumble of items lay in a heap at her feet. The hall tree measuring was forgotten.

All she could do at first was just sift through the things on the floor and sort them into piles. Then she did the same thing with the rest of the items remaining in the closet. She removed all the hanging things and laid them on the couch in the living room. She emptied the shelf at the top of the closet. And after scooping up all the stuff on the closet floor, and sorting those items into piles, she swept out the rest. Then, she did a once-over of all she'd accomplished so far, trying to determine how to put the things back in, which items could go, and which should be stored elsewhere.

She made short mental work of that task and went after the boxes first.

She had already placed three boxes on the shelf when she

decided that a large shoebox could fit on top of them. Trouble was, she was probably too short to reach up there, since the closet ceiling was as tall as the ten-foot ceilings of the old house. But she figured if she got one edge up then jumped and gave the thing a little shove, it would slide in nicely.

She was wrong. It didn't.

The box tumbled down on top of her and Sammi jumped backward, twisting her ankle a bit in the process as she and the box and its contents landed outside the closet door.

Sammi exhaled and surveyed the mess while she rubbed her ankle. "Well. Let's just clean this up," she said aloud as she picked up papers and envelopes and started shoving them back in the box.

A sweet, floral scent drifted up from the letters. She glanced down at the feminine handwriting on the linen envelopes, which were all addressed to Caleb here, at his North Carolina address. A quick look at the return address told her the letters came from an S. Weatherly in Montana. And S. Weatherly, Sammi surmised, was most definitely a woman.

Her curiosity piqued, Sammi continued to scrutinize the letter, wondering who S. Weatherly could be, when she realized the postmark date of the letter in her hand was barely two weeks old.

Something clutched at Sammi that she didn't want to acknowledge. It didn't mean anything, she told herself, but her mind raced. The mystery woman had written a letter to Caleb about the same time he'd asked her to marry him.

Who was S. Weatherly? And why was she writing Caleb perfumed letters?

She turned it over and noticed the broken seal. Sighing, Sammi glanced around her at the other papers and things on the floor. There were more letters. When she gathered them up and counted them, there were twenty-two, dating back to mid-winter, and coming regularly.

Sammi bolted upright in panic as she heard Caleb hammer the new shingles to the roof above her. Something sickening roiled up from deep in her belly, and she hated it. She should have known. Everything was too perfect.

Did she really know Caleb? Did she know him at all?

She knew little about his past, why he had come here, and what kinds of relationships he'd had before. No, she realized, she didn't know him at all.

The perfume burned her nostrils, and Sammi glanced back into her hands at the most recent letter, postmarked just a few weeks ago. Above her, Caleb continued to hammer. She wasn't sure why she did it, because it was a very uncharacteristic thing for her to do, but she slipped the letter out of the envelope and opened it.

Dear Caleb,

I need to see you. I cannot wait until we are together again. I want you to know that I've left my husband. I will join you soon. I live for the day that I can lie in your arms again and hold you deep into the night. I miss your touch how you make me feel. I long for the time that we will be together, without all the troubles here.

It won't be long, Caleb. But until then, my love....
Susan

THE DISGUST SAMMI FELT THEN, DEEP INSIDE HER gut, almost made her physically ill. S. Weatherly was Caleb's lover, a lover he'd never mentioned, a lover who was planning to join him.

Did she know about her? Had Caleb told her he was

getting married? Did Caleb really plan to marry her? After all, he had proposed on a whim, when her mother got ugly.

Does he really want to marry me? Oh, God....

No, Sammi thought, she didn't know Caleb at all. With that, numbness settled over her as she haphazardly shoved the letters back in the box, crammed on the lid, and pushed it into the closet. After that, she tossed back every single item in front of her with frenzied speed. She didn't want Caleb to know that she'd been in the closet and found the letters. She didn't want him to know what she knew.

And Sammi knew she was going to fall apart. And when that happened, she didn't want to be anywhere near Caleb. She didn't want to hear him lie about what she already knew, that he was in love with someone else, not her. She was just a diversion until this Susan, whoever she was, stepped back into his life.

As the back door slammed and she made her way toward her car, she heard Caleb shout from the roof. She didn't turn to look at him or acknowledge his presence.

She simply got in her car and drove home. And until she figured this thing out, that was where she intended to stay.

THREE HOURS LATER, SAMMI AWOKE IN HER BED, feeling groggy and disoriented. She remembered driving home —it was the longest fifteen minutes of her life. And she remembered unlocking the back door and holding Dicey for a bit while she tried to keep from falling apart. The fifteen-minute span between her home and Caleb's was just enough time for her to realize that she could never get back what they had shared.

She didn't trust him.

And if he knew she'd read the letter, he wouldn't trust her, either. It was a moot point, anyway. If she couldn't trust him, there would be no relationship. All the nights of making love, all the times he'd showered her with attention and affection and told her how wonderful their life would be, meant nothing now. He didn't love her. He had a lover somewhere else.

Try as she might to keep herself together, she couldn't, and somehow, she found her way to the bedroom and had cried herself to sleep. Now, pushing up to sit on the edge of the bed, Sammi looked in the dresser mirror across the room and saw that she not only felt but also looked a total mess.

A noise from the kitchen startled her. It sounded like her back door opening.

"Sammi?"

She cringed at the voice and fell back down against the bed, burying her face in her pillow. No. Not now.

But the footsteps grew louder, and she knew they were coming down her hallway and that, within seconds, they would be at her door.

"Sammi! Are you sleeping?"

She felt like lying there and not responding, hoping her mother would go away. Then she felt her mother's weight shift the mattress a bit, as she sat down and placed a hand on Sammi's shoulder.

"Sammi, wake up. I want to talk to you. I'm thinking of going away for a few days and was wondering if you could—" Her mother poked her again.

"I'm awake," Sammi said finally.

"Then turn around here and look at me so I can talk to you."

Sammi sighed and did. She didn't care.

"As I was saying—My God! What has happened to you?"

Sammi knew her face was swollen and her eyes puffy. She looked a mess, and right now, she didn't care.

"I've been crying, Mother. Isn't that obvious? Now, what do you need me to do? Tell me and then let me get some sleep."

Her mother stared for what seemed a terribly long time. Sammi waited.

"Is this about Caleb? I told you not to let yourself get hurt, Sammi."

Sammi bristled. "I didn't let myself, Mother. It just happened."

"Tell me what the problem is."

"There is no problem. There is no engagement."

Sammi glanced down at her finger, then quickly removed the ring. "Caleb and I are not getting married."

"Why?" her mother quickly returned.

"Because he's in love with another woman."

"I don't believe that."

Sammi forced her gaze up to her mother's face. "Why do you say that?"

"Because I've seen him around you. He loves you."

"But there is something you don't know, Mother. He has —someone in Montana. A woman."

Her mother's gaze narrowed, and Sammi felt under scrutiny. "Is that a problem?"

Sammi's heart almost stopped beating. "Yes, that is a problem!"

Her mother rose off the bed and stepped toward the dresser. Sammi watched Desiree's face in the mirror. Her mother was looking down, thoughtful, tracing her finger over the polished wooden frame of the mirror. Then she lifted her eyes to meet Sammi's in the reflection.

"You have to make the ultimate decision here, Sammi, but I'm going to give you a piece of advice. Please listen to me.

"Caleb seems to love you. However, you're not the woman anyone would call beautiful. You're practical, you're efficient, you're stable. And you're somewhat attractive. What I'm saying, Sammi, is that you are wife material."

Sammi winced, not sure she wanted her mother to go on.

"Caleb knows that, Sammi. You could be the perfect wife for him, take care of his home and bear his children and be there for him in business and home life. However, remember this." Her mother's stare in the reflection was becoming quite forceful now, as if to drive her point home. "Caleb will seek other women. So what? All men are like that, Sammi. A plain wife like you is safe. A beautiful woman is tempting. So, it's something you must learn to accept, or you shouldn't get married. Ever."

Staring at her mother's reflection, Sammi felt so much disgust she didn't quite know how to handle it. She felt her heart beating faster. "I can't accept it, Mother, because I don't believe a word you're saying."

"You don't believe Caleb has a lover?" her mother retorted.

"I don't believe the theory behind what you are saying. Whether or not Caleb has a lover, I don't know. But I won't live in a marriage like that."

"Don't be dumb, Sammi. The man will have a lucrative veterinary practice here someday."

"I won't marry for money."

Her mother's brows arched. "And what's that supposed to mean?"

Sammi rose off the bed. "It means that I won't stay with Caleb unless I know I'm the only woman in his life. I could never marry a man just so I can hope that he'll die someday, and I can have his money. Never."

Desiree lifted her chin and stared into her daughter's face. "In other words, you don't want to end up like me."

"You are exactly right."

Desiree stood there, looking at her for a few seconds, then

nodded. "I understand, Sammi," she whispered. "I wish I'd had your strength and conviction when I was your age." She stepped forward and gently placed her fingers under Sammi's chin, angling her face upward. "Go for the happy ending, honey. I hope you get it. I never could."

With that, her mother left, and Sammi burst into tears. Again.

THE NEXT MORNING, SAMMI WINCED AS THE CLINIC door behind her closed with a soft click. She didn't move but continued to type new patient information into the computer. Caleb had three appointments that morning, so they had barely spoken because of a lack of time. In between times, he'd darted in and out trying to finish patching the roof, telling Sammi that rain was on its way and he had to get that task finished.

She just kept on working, tossing him half-smiles and a few comments here and there as he rushed by. He'd even kissed her on the cheek as he grabbed some coffee before his first appointment but disappeared again just as quickly. Sammi was glad. It was hard to put up the pretense that everything was okay when it wasn't.

Everything was definitely not okay.

Now, she hoped he was heading back to the roof.

"Ready for lunch?"

Sammi glanced at her watch. It was nearly that time. Turning, she looked at him fully for the first time that morning. His smile nearly melted her, as always, until she remembered the perfumed letter; the lingering smell of it still made her a bit nauseated.

"I think I'll skip lunch today." She turned back to the computer.

Caleb grasped the back of her chair and swung her around. He crouched on the floor in front of her, his face eye-level with hers. "Oh, no you don't. Skip lunch? That's not good for you."

Leaning forward, he nuzzled her ear, placing his lips there and planting soft kisses down her neck.

Sammi wondered if he did that to Susan.

She put her hands on his chest and pushed, her chair hitting the computer table with a thud. She hadn't meant to push that hard. "I don't want lunch, Caleb." What she had wanted to say was *I don't want you to do that.*

Caleb's expression seemed a puzzled surprise. He sat back on his haunches, his fists resting on his thighs. "Okay, no lunch then. Do you mind if I eat?"

Sammi turned back to face the computer. "No, Caleb, why would I mind if you eat? I just have work to do."

Caleb stood. "So in other words, leave me alone, Caleb. Go away."

Sammi closed her eyes. This was impossible.

"I didn't mean it like that."

"Then how did you mean it?"

"I simply meant to say—"

He twirled her chair around again. "Sammi, talk to *me,* not the computer." His eyes bored into hers. "Now, what's wrong?"

Her mouth suddenly went dry. "Wrong?"

Caleb cleared his throat and glanced off. After a second, he crouched down again in front of her. "Sammi, you left here yesterday without a word. You didn't call me last night. When I called you, you cut the conversation short. This morning you've been cold and indifferent and have barely spoken a dozen words to me. Just this minute you pushed me away and snapped at me. Something is wrong, and I want to know what it is."

Sammi held the connection between them for a few seconds longer, then looked away. A muscle in her neck twitched. Her breathing was coming in erratic spurts. She wasn't sure she could trust her voice right now. And if pushed, she might break into tears.

But she was determined. She would get through this. She had decided, deep into the night, that this was the best way.

"Caleb, we need to talk."

He slowly nodded. "Obviously."

Her gaze drifted downward to her hands in her lap. Almost involuntarily, she reached to her finger and removed the engagement ring. She knew he was watching. When her gaze lifted to his face, and her eyes connected with his again, she saw the question there. She bit the inside of her lip and handed him the ring.

"I'm breaking the engagement, Caleb," she said softly. "I can't marry you. And I can't work for you anymore."

Chapter Fourteen

Caleb watched her go.

To say he was damned confused was an understatement. What just happened here?

Sammi's engagement ring dug into his palm, his hand clutching it tightly in his fist. He couldn't believe it. They'd made plans, made love, made more plans, and made love again. This made little sense.

He brought the ring closer to his face. Light reflected off every facet of the diamond. It wasn't an enormous stone, but the setting was unique and beautiful. Sammi was ecstatic when he'd chosen that one for her. She'd selected a much plainer style. He'd told her he wanted her to have a ring as unique and beautiful as she herself was.

And now, for some reason she wouldn't explain, she didn't want it. And she didn't want him.

Slowly, Caleb turned and headed for the house. It was going to rain.

THE STORM POUNDED IN HER EARS. THROUGHOUT the night it seemed, thunder rolled, and lightning split the sky. From beneath her covers, Sammi drifted in and out of consciousness, aware of the storm, and aware that something just wasn't quite right.

Finally, she awoke, listening. And then she realized.

Dicey.

The cat hated storms. Whenever it thundered at night, the animal curled up next to her on the bed. Sammi had never minded, not a lover of storms herself. The cat was always comfort. That was what was wrong now—Dicey was missing. Sammi wracked her brain trying to remember the last time that she'd seen the cat. She had come in after dinner, hadn't she?

Sammi remembered letting her out, as usual, earlier that evening. Dicey loved to explore and play outside, and usually came back home bearing a gift of a dead mouse, a mole, or a tiny bird—which generally grossed her out, until Caleb told her one day it was Dicey's way of showing Sammi love.

Caleb. Since she'd left the farm earlier in the day, she'd felt lost in an emotional fog. And right now, she couldn't remember if she'd let Dicey back inside.

Throwing back the covers, she left the bed and headed for the kitchen. After flipping on the back porch light, she opened the door. Peeking outside, she looked for any sign of the animal in the dark, although it was difficult to see with the wind and rain blowing in under her porch roof. She was sure that if Dicey were on the porch, she would have rushed in the door. The cat either had to be in the house or taking shelter from the storm somewhere else.

She shut the door and turned off the light. Standing there in the dark, Sammi wondered where to look. She headed through the house, then heard a faint meowing sound coming from the spare bedroom.

"Oh my goodness! My poor Dicey!"

Sammi rushed into the room. Dicey was lying in the center of the spare twin bed, her body heaving as she panted. She meowed long and low and looked up at Sammi, as if asking for help.

Sammi slowly approached her. She sat on the edge of the bed and laid a soft hand on Dicey's bulging belly. "Does it hurt, girl?"

Dicey meowed weakly.

Sammi withdrew her hand. The kittens were coming, and she did not know what to do.

SOMETHING COLD HIT CALEB ONCE IN THE FACE, then again. Unconsciously, he rubbed it away. Then it came back. Again.

Opening his eyes, Caleb looked up at the ceiling, almost in time to see another drip come careening down toward his face. He rolled, and the water splattered onto his pillow, immediately soaking into the cotton pillowcase.

"Damn."

He surveyed the ceiling once more, then looked back at the bed. The thing was too huge to move out of the way. He needed to find something big enough to catch the drips. Tripping down the stairs to the kitchen, he fetched a large stockpot and raced back again to place it between the pillows. Time to deal with the leaky roof.

But he'd be a fool to go up there now. The storm seemed to have subsided a bit, the thunder and lightning had ceased, and all he really wanted to do was get up there and see exactly where the problem was, so he would know where to start in the morning.

Besides, he had nothing else to do, and it was the middle of the night. He obviously couldn't sleep in his bed, so he might as well see about the roof.

He quickly dressed, then headed downstairs. "Now where is that rain slicker?" He mumbled as he headed toward the mudroom at the back of the house, then halted and snapped his fingers. Last time he'd seen it was in the entry closet.

Retracing his steps, he approached the closet and opened the door but found it too dark to see inside. He flipped on the light switch.

"My God, this closet is a mess."

Then reality dawned on him. "I know I'm a slob, but I don't remember the closet being *this* messy."

He glanced through the haphazardly tossed items, open boxes, and other sundry items. "Funny, how did these things get spilled—"

Something wasn't right. Crouching, he sifted through the items, a funny feeling settling over him. He grasped a handful of envelopes and...letters.

The letters.

My God. She found the letters from Susan.

An uncommon panic rushed over him.

Frantically, he pushed through the stuff until he found the box, its lid half-off. The letter on top, the most recent one he'd received, was sticking partly out of the envelope. He knew he hadn't left it like that.

In fact, he hadn't even read it. He had read none of them. He was nearly tempted two weeks ago to read the last one and had opened the flap on the back to do so, but had resisted. The only reason he'd wanted to read it was to see what was on Susan's mind. And the only reason he'd kept the letters was that someday he hoped to use them against her, as evidence, if need be.

It was a stupid thing to do. He should never have kept them.

Leaning against the closet door, Caleb heaved out a long breath. Sammi had been in here, he was sure. The day she'd left so quickly, she'd been inside the house for a while. He knew what had happened. Over the last few days, she'd been going through things, straightening, organizing, and cleaning. He hadn't minded, she was just being Sammi.

Obviously, while in her *let's-organize-Caleb's-life* mood, she'd hit upon the closet.

God, he was an idiot.

Looking down at his shaking fingers, he slipped the letter from the envelope and read it for the first time. Then he knew with certainty that Susan Weatherly had lost her mind.

The trouble in Montana had followed him to Harbor Falls.

SAMMI RACKED HER BRAIN, TRYING TO THINK OF anything she'd ever heard or seen about animals giving birth. All she could remember was that if things went right, everything should take care of itself.

She would have Googled it, but the power went out with the storm.

How would she know if things were going right?

And if some things went wrong, what would happen to her poor Dicey?

Would it be possible for kittens to come out backwards or sideways or something? Or feet first, like human babies sometimes did? Then what? And what if they wouldn't come out at all? What would she do then?

Dicey yowled, an unnerving sound that escalated with each contraction. Her body heaved a couple of more times, shook a little, and with another yowl, Sammi noticed the first kitten emerging.

She sat transfixed on the edge of the bed, her flashlight fixed on Dicey, as she watched the miracle of the tiny birth take place before her. Finally, one shiny, slick little newborn kitten slipped out of Dicey and into the world.

Dicey mewed what sounded like a tired sigh and nudged the kitten closer to her belly. She licked its face, then looked up again to Sammi. The cat stared at her for a moment, then the heaving of her body started again.

It was only a few minutes later when another kitten was born, and Sammi found herself able to move.

She stood up. This was too wonderful, too exciting, just too....

"MmmmmEEEEEEEOOOOOOOwwwwwww!"

Sammi looked at her cat. Suddenly, the animal seemed panic-stricken. She rolled a little. She twisted and yowled once again, and her body shook.

Sammi panicked and raced through the dark for the house phone.

Dead. No service.

She prayed she'd charged her cell phone.

CALEB DECIDED THERE WAS NOTHING HE COULD DO now, in the middle of the night, about the letters. Sammi would be asleep. No use waking her to tell her the truth about the entire Susan Weatherly affair.

Which it wasn't. An affair.

No, morning was best. By then, he hoped he'd have a better handle on how to explain all this to Sammi, why he hadn't ever mentioned it, and convince her, one last time, that she was the only woman for him, for all the remaining days of his life.

He knew this had hurt her. And likely her self- esteem,

which was just getting a good positive jolt, had been shot down again.

He would get to work on the roof. That was the task at hand. So once again he started for the door, after pulling on his rain slicker and boots, and headed into the night.

A flash of lightning in the distance warned him he probably shouldn't be up on the roof right now, but he waited for a few seconds, saw nothing else, took note that the rain had most likely passed, and put one foot on the ladder leaning against the house. He was three rungs up when he thought he heard the phone ring inside the house. He waited. One. Two. Three. Four rings. Then nothing. It was probably just someone with a silly minor problem, like a snoring hamster or something.

The clap of thunder boomed behind him about the same time the cell phone hooked to his belt rang. At that instant, he jumped, one foot slipping off the slick rung, and caught himself just in time as he tumbled backwards awkwardly, tripping and slipping down rung after rung until finally landing on his rear with a squish in the mud.

Dazed, Caleb shook his head and breathed in deeply to quell the fright inside him. Then the cell chimed again at his waist.

He fumbled with the thing and removed it from his belt, then pressed the key on the top to light up the number.

Sammi?

SAMMI RACED FOR THE DOOR WHEN SHE HEARD Caleb's knock. She'd already decided, moments earlier, that she was going to have to forget the trouble with Caleb right now and make sure that Dicey was safe.

She opened the door. "Oh, Caleb, thank you for coming. She's in here."

Caleb flipped the light switch by the door. "What's wrong with your lights?"

"Power's off. Come on!" She turned and hurriedly made her way back to the bedroom, flashlight leading the way, Caleb following behind. Stopping short of the bed, she pointed. "There."

She watched Caleb's face as he carefully approached the animal. Dicey mewed up at him and sniffed his hands. She growled a little as Caleb scratched her behind her ear.

"There, there, girl," he said in a soothing voice. "You're going to be alright."

"Is she okay?"

Caleb sat on the edge of the bed and ran his fingers along Dicey's belly. He gave her a quick once-over and looked back at Sammi. "Two kittens already?"

Sammi nodded. "She's in pain."

"She's giving birth, Sammi."

"Is she okay?"

Caleb nodded and assessed the situation. "There will be another, I think. She's fine. She knows what to do. I don't see any signs of distress."

"But it's been a while since the last one."

"She's resting. Give her time."

Sammi looked at her cat, worried. "So what do we do?"

Caleb rose and looked into her eyes. "We wait. We turn that flashlight off for a while. We watch her. Let her know we're here. Our presence is probably comforting to her. And we talk."

Sammi realized he wasn't referring only to Dicey's condition. He wanted to talk to her—and there would be no avoiding him.

"What do we talk about?" she whispered and lowered the

flashlight. Moonlight fell from the window onto the bed between them.

"Us. You and me. What happened yesterday?"

Sammi avoided Caleb's eyes. He sincerely wanted to talk, but she sure as hell wasn't up for it right now.

"MMMeeeeeeoooooowwwwwwWWWWWW!"

"Oh my! Dicey!"

They both turned their attention to the cat. She shuddered and let out another yowl as her body convulsed once more and slowly, slowly pushed out another kitten. Caleb moved gently toward the cat, and even though she let out a low growl at him, he carefully helped ease the kitten into existence.

"Goodness, this is a big one." Then he placed the kitten toward Dicey's nose, and she nudged it close to the others. In mid-lick, she suddenly yowled again and very quickly, another newborn kitten made its way into the world.

"I hope, Miss Dicey, this is the last of them." And within a few more minutes, it was apparent that all Dicey's litter had been born.

Caleb stepped back, and Sammi studied his profile while he watched the mama cat and let nature take over.

"Amazing, isn't it?"

At first, Sammi wondered what he was talking about, then followed his gaze to the new little family before her. Dicey was busy cleaning her brood, oblivious to those surrounding her.

"Perhaps we should leave her alone now," Sammi suggested.

Caleb looked at her. "Yes, I think it's time we did that. I think it's time we move on to another matter entirely."

At once, the lights in the house flickered and came back to life. For the first time in hours, as she looked at Caleb, Sammi realized how much she missed him. She licked her dry lips and let out a small sigh, looking deep into his eyes. It was now or never. They were going to have to talk.

"I suppose you're right."

She was ready to talk, but she wasn't ready to hear the entire story. She didn't want to know about S. Weatherly. But she figured it was best to get it over with and get on with her life.

"You're sure Dicey is okay?"

He nodded. "Believe me, she feels better. I don't know about you, but I could use a cup of coffee."

Sammi agreed. "You got it. Follow me."

"I think I know what happened yesterday," Caleb began a few minutes later, cradling a coffee mug in his hands.

"You do?" Sammi doubted it.

"I have a pretty good idea."

Sitting across from him at the table, she watched him reach in his pocket and pull out a piece of paper. He thrust it toward her. No, it wasn't paper; it was the letter.

The scent wafted up to her nose. Sammi glanced away.

"I think you found this yesterday."

She didn't want to look at him, and when she didn't answer, he leaned closer, reached out, and turned her face toward his. "Sammi, isn't that right?"

Deciding that she should fess up and be done with it, Sammi answered, "Yes."

"And you read it."

"Yes," she repeated.

"And from that you deduced I was having an affair with a woman from Montana."

Sammi lifted her chin and met his gaze. "Yes."

Caleb sighed and settled back down into his chair. "You should have asked me about this."

Not believing her ears, Sammi replied, "Excuse me? I

should have asked the man I was about to marry about his love letters from another woman?"

It was his turn to answer. "Yes."

Sammi sharply exhaled.

"So ask me."

"What?"

"Ask me."

The challenge of his gaze bore into hers.

"This is ridiculous," she replied.

"It's only ridiculous if we throw away our entire relationship on a misunderstanding because you refuse to ask me about those letters."

Sammi threw up her hands. "Why don't you just tell me, Caleb, instead of playing games?"

He studied her face. "All right. But you have to promise me you'll listen until the very end."

She reluctantly nodded her agreement. "Just tell me. I...I want to know."

He paused for a moment. "All I ever wanted, Sammi, was a home, a family, someone to love, and someone to love me back. Ever since my parents died, that had been my dream. My aunt and uncle were good providers, and they loved me, but it wasn't the same. So, I worked extremely hard for several years, going to school, getting my veterinary degree, and starting my practice in a local clinic near Bozeman, in order to achieve that dream.

"Things were going well for me. I worked for several years at the clinic, then the opportunity came for me to buy into it, to become a part owner. I really felt that this was going to lead me to achieve my dream. I wanted a small ranch, a home, and I wanted a wife and family. For some crazy reason, I thought I had to have them in that order. I wanted to have a home established before I settled down with the right woman.

"I approached the owner of the clinic and told him I was

interested. He said great, and we started working out the details. I went to the bank to see if I could get the funds. I figured I was home free. There was only one problem."

He looked into her face, and Sammi peered deep into his eyes. "And what was that?"

"Susan Weatherly."

"Oh."

"Susan Weatherly was the wife of the man who owned the clinic, the other vet in the practice—the man I'd be sharing the business with. Susan Weatherly had come on to me several times. She told me she didn't love her husband, and she wanted to have an affair with me."

"An affair?"

He nodded. "She didn't want to leave her husband—he provided for her nicely. She just wanted some side action, apparently."

"And you said...?"

"I put her off time and time again, but when she realized I wanted to buy into the business, she came back. I refused her again. She was so angry that I'd jilted her she vowed to get back at me—and she did."

Sammi watched Caleb's face turn from relaxed to rigid as he told the story. Studying his eyes, she realized that this man in front of her, this man she loved, was not making up a story or telling her a lie. Emotion was etched across his face, and the hurt he must have gone through then was coming back to him now.

"What did she do?" Sammi softly questioned.

Caleb grasped Sammi's hand and drew her closer. He rubbed the back of her knuckles as he continued. "She told everyone she knew, including her husband, that we were lovers, that we'd been romantically involved for some time."

"She told her husband?"

"Yes, she told him. Of course, the deal was void after that. I was the laughingstock of the entire community. My aunt and uncle were ashamed, although they believed that what I told them was the truth.

"Of course, I lost my job, and even though I probably could have fought it, I didn't. By that time, I was ready to get out of there and strike out on my own. So that's what I did, and that's how I ended up here."

Sammi found she was leaning forward, listening to Caleb's story, holding on to his every word. But she needed more. He hadn't explained everything yet.

"But what about the letters, Caleb?"

He shrugged. "Susan was a little unstable. Everyone knew that. Even though she was well- liked, attractive, and an upstanding member of the community, she had some problems. She drank too much which people mostly overlooked, and she had affairs, which many people knew about. But when she couldn't have me, it threw her for a loop. She started sending letters to my old address, then the first few were forwarded here—and from there, she obviously got hold of my new address.

"Until today, I'd read none of those letters. When I finally realized you had found them yesterday, I read the one you have in your hand. That's when I understood why you had broken off our engagement—you thought I was having an affair with this woman.

"And knowing you the way I do, I know you wouldn't accept a situation like that. Am I right?"

Sammi nodded her agreement. "Yes, Caleb, that's what I thought. And yes, you're right. It would not be acceptable."

He pulled both her hands closer so he could kiss her fingers. "Sammi," he whispered. "I have never lied to you, nor will I. I was never Susan Weatherly's lover. She feels the need to make my life miserable because I rejected her. I am not in love with Susan Weatherly and never have been. I am in love with you."

Sammi wanted so much to believe him, and she did—but yet, she needed one more thing from him, one more answer.

"Why did you keep them?"

He shook his head and sighed. "For some crazy reason, I thought that by keeping the letters I would have some proof of her unbalanced behavior. That's why I shoved them to the back of the closet. That's the only reason I kept them."

"Why didn't you have them stopped?"

"I don't know. I guess I just didn't want to deal with it. I thought about it, but the past few months I've been so busy I never got around to doing anything about it. Besides, the memories were just too painful. Once I was here, rebuilding my life, trying to get on with my dream, I didn't want any interference. I wanted to be alone. So, when the letters came, I simply tossed them in the box in the closet—out of sight, out of mind.

"I know I need to deal with this situation. In fact, what I have to do is gather up all the letters and send them back to Montana to a friend of mine who's a police lieutenant. I think if he makes it clear to her that what she's doing is harassment, she will stop this. And tomorrow that's what I intend to do."

Sammi closed her eyes and leaned back. "I believe you, Caleb," she whispered.

It took only a split second for him to push out of his chair and wrap his arms around her, pulling her close to him. His hand went to her neck. "I want you, Sammi, only you. I love you. And I promise you will be the only woman I will love, the only woman I will make love to, for the rest of my life. You are so beautiful to me. I have absolutely no desire to have anyone else."

He pulled her face up to his and then kissed her, softly, tenderly. Sammi felt the love and desire and passion she'd always felt for him well up from deep inside her. Caleb wrapped his arms tightly around her. He held her so tight that she knew—

The cat meowed.

Sammi and Caleb both turned. Laughing, Sammi grabbed his hand and started pulling him toward the cry. "Let's go see what she wants."

"Damned cat is practically ruling the roost, isn't she?"

Sammi smiled crookedly and leaned onto his shoulder. "You better believe it."

They entered the room and located the cat family. Dicey stared at them, gazing at the couple as if to say, *Well, it's about time. Look what I have!*

"Oh my, look at them, Caleb!" Sammi exclaimed.

The four previously wet newborn kittens, now licked clean, were partially fluffed and mewling. She and Caleb watched as the four fur balls struggled to nurse at Dicey's belly. The mama cat nudged each of them along a bit, then looked back at her visitors.

"Strange colors, those kittens," Caleb remarked.

Sammi nodded. "Two black and white, one yellow, and one looks like a calico, don't you think? Dicey must have played the field," she commented and grinned. "Is that possible? Flirty little feline."

Caleb chuckled and wrapped his arms around her. "She's the only one in this family allowed to play the field."

Sammi cocked her head to one side. "Is that right, Dr. Wyatt?"

"Yes, Ms. Jamieson. If you don't mind my saying so."

"I think I like the sound of that."

"I think I like the sound of that, too."

Caleb kissed her and, reaching into his pocket, pulled out the engagement ring, and slowly slipped it back onto her finger. "I love you, Sammi Jamieson. You are the most beautiful, most incredible woman in the world, do you know that?"

Sammi narrowed her gaze, and through misty eyes, tossed him an impertinent grin. "I'm still not sure. Tell me again."

"What? You need more convincing?"

Sammi lowered her hands to his waist and began unfastening his belt buckle. Oh, how very happy she was that she had taken a chance or two this summer. "Dr. Wyatt, not that I am insecure in our relationship, or anything, but I may require a lifetime of convincing."

And that was something that Caleb Wyatt didn't mind doing, not one bit. Convincing Sammi—day after day if he had to—that she was beautiful and loved and the most important person in his world, was his *forever* plan.

A Note from Maddie

Friends,

Thank you for reading *Convince My Heart*, Book 6 in my Falls Mountain Romance series!

I love this simple, small-town story of how Caleb and Sammi come to love each other. They had their complications, for sure, and were able to conquer them. So glad to send them on their way with a sweet happily-ever-after!

For more happily-ever-afters, check out my other Falls Mountain or Sweet Hart Inn books.

If you enjoyed this read, then please consider sharing with others. One of the best ways to tell others about the book is to leave a review at Goodreads, or at the bookstore where you purchased the book. You can also leave reviews at my website, maddiejamesbooks.com.

More Sweet Hart Inn

Cozy up at the inn where the heart of the Blue Ridge beats strongest...

Welcome to Sweet Hart Inn, a charming bed and breakfast nestled along the peaceful shores of Falls Lake, at the foot of Falls Mountain. At the center of it all is chef and innkeeper Suzie Hart, whose kitchen is always warm, and whose heart is always open. Together with her husband Brad, Suzie serves up matchmaking advice and comfort food, along with second chances, and a generous helping of happily ever after.

The Sweet Hart Inn Books

All of My Heart
Take My Heart
Match My Heart
Tame My Heart
The Dating Game
Miss Matched Hearts
The Husband List
Chase My Heart
No Sweeter Match
One More Kiss

The Falls Mountain Books

Welcome to Falls Mountain, and the quaint town of Harbor Falls.

Tucked deep into the Blue Ridge Mountains, bricked streets, lakeside views, and charming local shops set the scene for small town romance.

In this standalone-but-interconnected series, you'll meet bakers, bookstore owners, chocolatiers, school teachers, and more—all trying to run their businesses, chase their dreams, and keep their hearts in check. But in Harbor Falls, love has a habit of showing up unannounced...

From second chances to secret babies to grumpy-sunshine pairings, each book brings a satisfying happily-ever-after and a cast of characters you'll want to visit again and again.

Falls Mountain Romance is a companion series to the Sweet Hart Inn Romance books by Maddie James.

Dance into My Heart
The Christmas Nanny
The Heartbreaker

Star Crossed
Not This Christmas
Convince My Heart

I hope you'll check out these books, and my other series, on
my website at:
www.maddiejamesbooks.com

About Maddie James

Romance with a pulse—small towns, big love, and a dash of drama.

Maddie James writes small-town romance with heart, heat, and the occasional haunting. Her stories range from sweet to spicy, suspenseful to supernatural—happily-ever-afters guaranteed! From stand-alone love stories to binge-worthy series, Maddie delivers love next door, some cowboy kisses, an occasional hint of danger, and just enough drama to keep things interesting.

Get all the drama delivered to your inbox when you sign-on to Maddie's VIP reader list!
Free books, sneak peaks, bonus content, giveaways, and more...
Learn more: maddiejamesbooks.com/pages/newsletter